TO L

It All

Began

with a Goodbye

– A NOVEL –

*Thank you for all
the help & love you have
given me.*

Robin L.R. Kellogg

*Love,
Robin LR Kellogg*

NEWMAN SPRINGS PUBLISHING
320 Broad Street
Red Bank, NJ 07701

First originally published by Newman Springs Publishing 2023

Photo by Larry Estrin

ISBN 978-1-68498-643-9 (Paperback)
ISBN 979-8-89061-991-4 (Hardcover)
ISBN 978-1-68498-644-6 (Digital)

Printed in the United States of America

 DEDICATION

To my mother, who encouraged my interest in writing; I will always be grateful for her patience, compassion, strength, and love that she freely gave to her family, friends, and anyone else who came into her orbit.

CHAPTER 1

The Homecoming

"**O**h Sugar! What does he want?" *Did I just say that out loud?* Sarah looked around to see if her coworker Rita heard her. She was the only other employee at Thomas Finance Co. in Clifton, New Jersey, where Sarah had worked for the past year, since graduating from high school.

It was 1947, and the economy was booming. Sarah was still unaccustomed to this economic stability, having been born a year and a day before the Great Depression began on October 29, 1929. Her whole childhood had revolved around hardship and rations. World War II opened more stateside job opportunities, but the war also took her eldest brother, Nate, away from the family for a few years. Thankfully, he was home again.

"Are you okay, Sarah?"

Darn, Rita had heard her. "I'm fine. I just got word from the devil himself," said Sarah, staring at the telegram in her hand.

"Just remember the devil only has power over you when you give it to him. Let me know if you need anything, a baseball bat, blunt object, or someone to break his knees."

"I will," Sarah giggled. Her friendship with Rita was an unexpected but pleasant surprise. Rita had worked for Mr. Thomas for the past seven years, first part-time and then, as the economy improved, full-time.

When Sarah had first joined the team, Rita seemed standoffish. As soon as Sarah had broken the ice by sharing some of her family troubles, Rita had also loosened up and talked about her hardships: losing her husband during the war and how for several years she had worked two jobs to support her three young children. She had become a great sounding board for Sarah and understood the burden of having so much responsibility at a young age.

Sarah's father, Henry Steinman, had sent the telegram. Henry lived in Washington, D.C. Under normal circumstances, Sarah would bid him good riddance and be done with it, but Henry possessed something she had been trying to retrieve for two years: her youngest brother, Steven. Henry had taken Steven, with him, to live in D.C. when he married his second wife, Barbara. Sarah's mother, Rose, died back in 1940 of complications from kidney disease. There were whispers that it was the big C (cancer), but doctors had never confirmed it. In the end, her mother died, and the cause didn't matter, but the fact remained that she was gone.

Despite Sarah's multiple attempts to reach out to her absent father, he ignored her. She never expected much from Henry and wasn't completely surprised by his silence. But you could have knocked her over with a feather when she read his telegram, which arrived shortly after 3:00 p.m. on this very day.

Steven. STOP. Arriving 5PM train. STOP. Passaic Depot Station. STOP.

Why was he sending Steven back? Did it matter? She made a quick phone call to her Bubbe to let her know about Steven's imminent arrival. Sarah lived with her grandmother, her eldest brother, Nate, and her middle brother, David.

"Allo. Sarah, are you okay? Vhat's vrong?"

"Nothing is wrong, Bubbe. Everything is right. Steven is coming home!"

"Oy gevalt! HaShem has heard my prayers. I knew the good Lord vould bring my baby back to me. I'll make Steven's favorite meal. Vait until Nate and David find out!"

Sarah's joy spanned ear to ear. Her grandmother, Molly Roth, had landed at Ellis Island back in 1905, to join her husband, Lezer, short for Eliezer. He had come to America from Wysoki Litowsk, in Grodno, a part of the former Russian Empire. Despite her more than forty years in the US, her grandmother's Eastern European accent was ingrained into every syllable she uttered.

Sarah's next call was to Mitzi, her childhood best friend. Mitzi's full name was Mary Elizabeth Buckingham, but family and friends had always called her Mitzi. Sarah hoped her friend, who had a car, could be at the train station, as her backup, in case she was late.

"Hi, it's Sarah. You won't believe this. Henry is sending Steven back on the 5:00 p.m. train."

"Oh my goodness. You better hurry, Sarah. That's just over an hour from now!"

"I know. Do you think you can wait for him until I get there? If you can't, I'll understand…"

"Sarah, hang up the phone and get on the bus now. I'll go right over to the station so he won't be alone."

She owed her best friend a great deal. Mitzi was a friend Sarah could always count on. She had been there during some of the most tumultuous times in Sarah's life, including her mother's death. Sarah didn't know how she would ever repay her. Scribbling a quick note for Mr. Thomas, Sarah said, "Good night!" to Rita, grabbed her coat, and ran out the door.

By some miracle, she made it to the station with minutes to spare, despite having to take two buses to get there. She could hear the train coming down the tracks in the distance and saw Mitzi standing on the platform waiting. Though her friend's back was to her, Sarah could identify Mitzi by her bright, red wool coat and long, silky-straight chestnut hair. Sarah always admired her best friend's luxurious hair, having a mop of wavy, frizzy dull-brown hair herself.

Running up to her, she tapped Mitzi on the shoulder. As the train rolled into the station, Mitzi grabbed Sarah's hand. They stood as a united front waiting for Steven—his very own welcome home committee. When the train stopped and the stairs were put in place so passengers could disembark, the doors slid open, and Sarah saw

Steven. He was several inches taller than she remembered. Then again, he was nine when he left, and now he was eleven. He wore a suit that looked like it was two sizes too big for him, and he needed a haircut. The battered suitcase that he had left New Jersey with was by his side. But none of that mattered now. Steven was home.

"Steven! Steven!" Jumping up and down, Sarah waved her arms at her brother. When Steven saw her, his eyes lit up, and he ran toward her and gave her a big bear hug.

"Sarah! I'm so glad to see you. I missed you and Bubbe and Nate and David. I wasn't sure if I would ever see you again."

"We missed you too, kiddo." Sarah's voice was cracking as she held back tears.

"Let's go, you two. You both have had your share of public transportation for the day. I'm driving you home now." Holding Steven's hand in hers, Sarah kissed Mitzi on the cheek and whispered, "Thank you."

On the ride home, Steven appeared confused. He remembered the direction home, and this wasn't it.

"Aren't we going to the house, Sarah?"

The house. The house where he spent the first nine years of his life, where his memories had lived. "We live in an apartment building now. We moved there shortly after—after Henry took you to D.C."

Steven was pensive for the remainder of the ride and remained silent as they walked into the apartment. She would later find out that Henry had taken him out of school earlier that day without any explanation as to why. He had him change into the ill-fitted suit, made a quick stop at an attorney's office, and then he put Steven on a train headed for Passaic, New Jersey. Sarah assumed Henry made a stop at his lawyer's to make sure he could not be accused of abandonment. Funny, he didn't seem at all concerned about that when he left Sarah and her siblings a few short years after her mother's death.

As they reached the door to their apartment, Sarah realized that Steven had a good reason to be nervous. He was back with family he hadn't seen in two years, to a place that he had never called home.

CHAPTER 2

Reunited

The one thing that Sarah just couldn't get used to was how you could hear every step someone took on the stairs and in the hallway of their apartment building. It wasn't only the noise; it took away any chance of surprise.

Even before they reached the door, David opened it and popped his head out. "Remember me, squirt?"

Before Steven could answer his question, Bubbe pushed her way past David and ran out of the apartment with her arms spread wide. Steven was instantly swept up into Bubbe's arms, his head nestled between his grandmother's arms and her bosom.

"Oy, my bubbala. I'm so, so, so happy to see you. Steven, you're crying. Vhat's vrong, sweetheart?"

With tears rolling down his face, Steven said, "I've missed you too. I never thought I would see any of you again." Grabbing his grandmother around her waist, Steven began to sob.

Looking from Sarah to David, Molly could not begin to fathom what this little boy had gone through over the past two years. She'd make sure that from here on in he was well taken care of, loved, and that Henry was kept far away from him.

She lifted Steven's chin with her index finger. "Let me look at you. You have such a sveet punim, but ve have to fatten you up. Lucky for you, I've made a brisket vith potatoes."

"Mmm…my favorite. I love your brisket and potatoes. Did you bake any babka? I miss your babka too!"

Bubbe used the same recipe for her dessert as did her mother and her mother's mother. It was a tradition in their family. No matter what happened in life, you could always make babka.

Laughing, Molly put her hand on Steven's back and guided him to the table. "Come, sveetheart. Let's sit down and fress; you need to eat."

"But Nate's not here yet, Bubbe," said David.

"He'll be here shortly. Ve'll start vithout him."

A few minutes later, Nate poked his head into the kitchen. "Hey. Who's our dinner guest tonight?"

"That's Steven! Don't you recognize him?" asked David.

"Nah, that's not Steven. Steven's a little runt only about yea high," said Nate, bringing his hand to his waist. "This guy is bigger."

"It's me! It's me!" said Steven, jumping up and diving into Nate's open arms.

"I knew that, squirt! I was just razzing you. Welcome home, little brother!"

Dinner was delicious. Bubbe had outdone herself. Sarah looked around the table and was filled with joy. Her family was whole again. After Steven and David had gone to bed, Sarah sat on the sofa with her grandmother, her head on her chest, just as she had done as a little child.

"What are we going to do about Steven, Bubbe? Should I ask him about what happened while he was living with Henry these past two years, or should I leave it alone?"

"Let it be, for now. Steven vill talk vhen he's ready to talk."

In the days following Steven's return, Sarah came to realize that Bubbe was right. Steven would eventually talk about the time away when he was ready. In the meantime, she registered him for school and tried to make life as normal as possible for him. So far, no noise from Henry. Her last correspondence with him was that telegram.

CHAPTER 3

Henry's Return

S arah had tried her darndest to push any thoughts of Henry and her early childhood, with him, out of her mind. But Steven's return stirred up those old feelings of despair, anger, and fear.

She would never forget the day Henry walked through the front door of their home, after moving to Washington D.C. a year earlier.

It was a Sunday, a beautiful summer day. Sarah always left her chores for Sundays. She was too tired during the week after spending the day at school and going to work at her Uncle Jake's gas station for a few hours afterward. Then she had to help Bubbe make dinner, and Friday night through Saturday night was Shabbas. As observant Jews, Saturday was off-limits for any task.

Sarah was in her bedroom, near the back of the house, folding clothes. She was wearing a pair of her mother's shoes, something she did off and on. It reminded her of better times. It was considered a bad omen by the Jewish community to wear a deceased person's clothing, but Sarah didn't care. Just having the shoes on her feet made her feel connected to her mother.

She had left the front door open to air out the house, and the screen door unlatched, but closed. Bubbe had gone to her volunteer job at the Jewish Home, and her brothers were out with friends.

When she heard the screen door open, followed by footsteps, she assumed it was one of them returning home.

"I'll be right there." Sarah put down the laundry and made her way toward the living room. Walking down the hallway, she smelled it—Henry's favorite cologne. Stay calm. It can't be him. She repeated this statement to herself several times before she turned into the living room. There he was—her father, Henry, standing in the living room like a conquering sovereign who had come to survey his domain, his eyes moving to and fro, looking at their well-worn furniture and other belongings as if he were assessing their value.

Sarah glared at him. Hadn't he done enough harm to them already? She was only fifteen when he had abandoned them just a year earlier, leaving them nothing to live on. He had no conscience. He was their father, at least in the legal sense of the word, but she knew he had never cared about them. He made that evident every time he physically abused them, neglected their needs, and said things to demoralize them. He certainly wasn't the image of the typical Jewish father her Catholic friends had heard about, one who treasured his children and provided for them.

Henry donned a dress shirt, slacks and tie, and shiny leather dress shoes. Sarah wondered why the Almighty had allowed him to exist at all, a man who created so much misery for others. He wasn't wealthy by any stretch of the imagination, but he always had money for himself. Sarah could still see her poor mother, Rose, walking around in threadbare dresses while he had a closet full of clothes. Henry would say that he was the breadwinner, and it was important for him to dress well. Breadwinner! From Sarah's earliest recollections, it was her mother who opened, closed, and worked at the family's grocery store from dawn to dusk while Henry regularly disappeared from the store for hours at a time.

When Rose became ill and could no longer work, Henry closed the store but made sure to constantly remind her, and anyone else close enough to hear, that their strained financial situation was her fault.

Sarah's grandmother, Molly, moved in with them in 1937 to help run the household. Nothing was stopping her from caring for her daughter and grandchildren full-time, as her husband had died of a stroke several years earlier. Steven was crawling at the time and was getting into everything. Having her Bubbe there was a huge relief to everyone, except Henry. During the four years Molly took care of her daughter, Rose, and the household, Henry never spoke a word to her.

Ten months after Rose passed away, her brothers asked Henry if he had ordered the headstone for her upcoming unveiling ceremony. In typical fashion, he told the Roth boys that they could take care of it, adding that Rose was dead, and it was no longer his responsibility.

In 1943, Henry visited family in Washington, D.C. During that trip, he met Barbara, through a cousin. They married soon afterward. Henry left New Jersey without a care in the world.

Sarah could no longer stand the silence. She knew that standing up to Henry was going to mean war, but he had no right to be here any longer. He had abandoned them. Sarah wanted Henry out of her house now.

CHAPTER 4

Henry's Pronouncement

W hat are you doing here?" Sarah wanted him out, quick, but she was still a little curious as to why he was here in the first place.

Henry stood there, just staring at her, which only made Sarah seethe more.

"I asked you a question. What are you doing here?"

"I've come to tell you that Barbara and I have decided that having a rental in New Jersey is no longer a necessity for us.

"You don't have a rental. We do! We've been paying the rent, not you! Get—out—now!" Sarah stood with her arm stretched out, pointing toward the front door. She was shaking, and if she was aware of it, so was Henry. Predators always know when their prey is panicked.

"As usual, Sarah, you are missing the point. My name is on the lease. According to the law, I'm still the head of this household. So, I can do what I want, and I've decided that you, your brothers, and grandmother have thirty days to vacate the premises."

"That's impossible. I bet you're only doing this because you know Nate's still fighting in Europe. If he were home, he'd never allow you to do this, and you know it."

"Whatever my reasons are, Sarah, they do not include me being afraid of your brother, Nate! My name is on the lease, not his, not your uncles. I'm sure your grandmother and her sons will find a place for you all to live. Barbara and I have plans for the future, and they don't include any of you living here, as it poses tremendous liability. Start packing now. You've got thirty days."

Sarah was about to give Henry a piece of her mind when her grandmother walked through the door. Upon seeing the monster who had terrorized her daughter and abused her grandchildren, Bubbe screamed. "You killed my daughter, you mamzer! Get out of this house now!"

Sarah couldn't believe her ears. Her grandmother, who would yell at her for saying "heck," had just used a Yiddish curse word. Mamzer meant bastard—although it was an accurate description of her father.

"Watch your language, Molly. I didn't kill Rose. She died because her kidneys stopped working."

"You killed her in here," said Bubbe, pointing her hand toward her chest, "long before she died from that disease!"

"You don't want to cross me, Molly. I guess I lucked out that your perfect little daughter didn't have your temper. She just did whatever I told her to do until the day she died."

Molly stopped in her tracks. Even after all this time, she was unable to wrap her head around why Rose had stayed with Henry for as long as she did… HaShem, rest her soul.

"The difference between your daughter and you was that she knew her place and you don't. You could have taken some pointers from her, Molly," Henry said.

Sarah watched as her grandmother lunged for Henry, but he was too quick for her. He grabbed her by the shoulders and began shaking her. Sarah was terrified that he would kill her. It was bad enough that Henry had beaten Sarah and her brothers, but no one was going to touch her grandmother. Sarah grabbed Bubbe's large black umbrella from the stand near the door and began hitting Henry on the back of the head and about his body. He pushed Molly aside. Now his attention and anger were focused squarely on Sarah.

Taking a fistful of Sarah's hair, he pulled her forward, causing her to bend at the waist and stumble. Henry then caught her by the upper arm and held her against the wall, with his palm poised to meet her cheek. Sarah braced herself for the impact and then nothing. It wasn't like Henry to restrain himself like that.

Then she witnessed something so horrific, it would continue to haunt her dreams for some time. Her thirteen-year-old brother, David, who had just returned home after spending the afternoon with friends, had used his full body's weight and ran straight at Henry, elbows swinging every which way. David's actions took Henry by surprise, giving David the upper hand for a few precious seconds. Henry recovered quickly, however, and was able to grab onto the collar of David's shirt.

"You stupid runt. I'll show you what happens when you don't respect your elders," Henry said as he proceeded to land punches about David's head, chest, and back.

Sarah and Bubbe begged him to stop, but he needed something to hit, and David was that something. When Henry walked out of the door that day, David looked like a rag doll that had been dragged through the mud and run over by a truck. Sarah screamed after him, "You'll be sorry. I won't let you get away with this."

Sarah needed to get her brother to the hospital, but Bubbe asked her not to call an ambulance. It cost too much, and she was worried they might look like trouble, themselves, for causing such a disturbance. "What would the neighbors think?" So she did the next best thing and called Mitzi. Mitzi was still too young to have a driver's license, but her older brother, James, would always take them places. He dropped the three of them off at Beth Israel Hospital and told Mitzi he'd be back soon to pick them up. While the doctors were assessing and admitting David to the hospital, Sarah had a chance to tell her friend everything that had just happened.

"Are you kidding me, Sarah? Your father did that to David? And on top of it, he only gave you a month to find a new place? That's horrible! Every time your father did something in the past, my mother told me we all have faults and that I should find a redeeming quality about him, but this time, Sarah, this time he's gone too far. I feel so bad for you all."

David would spend the next week being treated for broken ribs, a fractured arm, and cuts and bruises. Upon Mitzi's advice, Sarah contacted the police about what her father had done to David, but they said this was a family dispute; he didn't break any laws. That angered Sarah. *When, if ever, would there be laws protecting children from abusive parents?*

CHAPTER 5

Weighing the Odds

The hospital bill was a few hundred dollars, a lot of money, money that they didn't have. However, her uncles assured Sarah they would take care of it. Henry should have paid for it, of course, but once again, he created chaos and then abandoned the consequences for someone else to deal with. While David was in the hospital, Bubbe and Sarah had started to look for a new place to live, and at least one seemed promising. They decided not to make a move for a couple of weeks until David had time to recover.

The day David was released from the hospital, Steven insisted on going with Uncle Robert to pick up him up. Robert was her grandmother's youngest child and the only one born in America. Sarah and Bubbe stayed behind to prepare for David's homecoming celebration. The entire family, which included her five uncles, their wives, and her cousins were expected to join them for dinner.

"I'll get it," Sarah told Bubbe after hearing a knock at the door. She opened it to find David still looking as though he had been through a war zone. He had cuts and bruises on his face, his torso was bandaged, and his arm was in a sling. Add to that, he was still a bit unsteady on his feet. Uncle Robert was holding him up on one side, and Steven was attempting to do the same on the other. Since

Steven was several inches shorter than David, it was comical to see him trying to keep David upright.

"Come on, David, let's get into bed," Uncle Robert said, as he lifted him in his arms and walked toward the bedroom David shared with Steven.

"But I want to see everyone when they come over," David fussed. "Don't worry," Uncle Robert said, "We'll bring you out to the living room when they show up."

Soon the house was flooded with family members who came with gifts and well-wishes for David. Uncle Robert kept his word and David was able to spend a little time with the family. However, after a half hour he was about to conk out. Uncle Robert carefully laid him in his bed.

Bubbe prepared a plate for David and asked Sarah to bring it to him. When Sarah entered the bedroom, David's eyes were closed, so she quietly placed the food on the nightstand and began to tiptoe toward the door.

"Thanks, Sarah."

"I thought you were asleep, David."

"I'm trying, but with everyone coming over, I'm too excited to sleep. Besides, I'm hungry."

"Aw, Buddy. I know you are. You still need to rest too, though. You've been through a lot. Bubbe will be glad you have an appetite. She's been cooking all your favorite dishes. You just eat what you can. When you're done eating, just yell, David. I'll come back and get your plate."

As she turned to leave the room, Sarah felt immense empathy for David. He had inherited Henry's temper and was also their father's favorite punching bag. She hoped that, one day, he would be able to get past this. Then again, she hadn't been entirely successful getting Henry out of her head either.

She heard David's voice once again. "Thanks, Sarah."

"You've already thanked me, David. I should be the one thanking you multiple times. I know you were trying to protect me from Henry. I'm so sorry you were hurt doing so."

"Thank you, but I mean it, Sarah—I know I can be a real pain in the neck sometimes, well, maybe a lot, and I want you to know how grateful I am that you're my sister. I know sometimes I have a temper, like Dad, but I'm not like him. I would never hurt my family."

Sarah stopped. David had spoken to her in such a mature way. She didn't want to patronize him. She was so proud of his newfound insight. It was almost too much to handle.

With tears in her eyes, she turned around to face David. "I am so proud of you, David. You have endured so much. You are my hero."

The smile on David's face shone brightly, despite the swollen, discolored appearance. "Hero, huh?"

"Yes, my hero. And don't you forget it," she said as she gently kissed David on his forehead.

"Yuck. Why'd you have to go and ruin it, Sarah?"

"I'm going to make believe you didn't say that," she said as she exited the room.

After Sarah, David, and Steven were out of earshot, the adults all whispered about taking legal action against Henry.

CHAPTER 6

The Court Challenge

David had been home from the hospital for several days when Dr. Cole, the family physician, stopped by the house to check on his progress.

"David will soon be running circles around you, once again, Mrs. Roth. If he develops a fever or has any other aches or pains, please give me a call."

When Bubbe tried to pay Dr. Cole for his services, he waved her hand away. Sarah's grandmother was a proud woman. She may not have had a lot of money, but she didn't take handouts either.

As Dr. Cole headed toward the door, Bubbe gave him a glass jar filled with fresh chicken soup and some babka wrapped in a cotton cloth.

"Hmm. It smells delicious, but you have to stop feeding me, Mrs. Roth. My wife is complaining I'm getting too fat."

Bubbe laughed and told him her chicken soup would help him to slim down. And as far as the babka went, everyone needed a little babka now and then.

Several minutes after Dr. Cole left, there was a knock on the door. "I'll get it, Bubbe. I bet the doctor forgot to tell you something." But to Sarah's surprise, it wasn't Dr. Cole but her uncles: Louie, Frank, Eddie, Jake, and Robert.

"Hi, come on in. What are you all doing here? Bubbe didn't mention you'd be stopping by."

As she walked her uncles into the living room, Sarah noticed that her grandmother had already taken a seat on the sofa.

"Sarah," Bubbe said, patting the seat cushion next to her. "Come. Sit. Ve need to talk."

"Did I do anything wrong?"

"No, sveetheart, nothing at all. Ve need to talk."

Sarah couldn't imagine what adult conversation would include her. Neither Bubbe, nor Sarah's uncles, had ever asked her to discuss anything of importance with them before.

Jake, Sarah's eldest uncle, spoke first. "Henry has gone too far this time. I should have taken care of this when Rose was still alive. For whatever reason, she stayed with that…"

"Jake," cautioned Bubbe. "Vatch your language in front of Sarah."

"Okay, okay." Jake continued. "We have to make sure he doesn't get a chance to hurt David or any of the kids again. Sarah, we wanted you to be here because we'd like you to consider something. Before we go into details, I want you to understand we've looked at all the angles, and this is the only truly feasible plan, the only one…"

"You've got to believe us, Sarah," her Uncle Frank interjected. "We would never ask you do this if…"

"He's right, Sarah. We love you all so much and only want the best for you," Eddie added. The brothers all shook their heads in agreement.

"We're only suggesting this because it's the best way to keep Henry out of your lives," added Robert.

Louis sat and absorbed everything his brothers and mother were saying to Sarah, but remained silent. He had a friend who might be able to help, but he wanted to mull this over before adding to the conversation.

"Let's not jump ahead of ourselves," Jake stated, trying to regain control of the conversation.

"Sarah, we've already discussed this with Mom, and we're all in agreement," Jake concluded.

"About what, Uncle Jake?"

"Oh, sorry… I…we think you and Mom should file for joint guardianship of David. We've discussed this matter with an attorney, and it's our understanding there's a good chance the court will agree with us and rule that Henry is an unfit parent."

Sarah looked at her uncle as if he had grown another head. "I'm not sure I understand how. I'm sixteen. I'm not even an adult. I also don't want to make Henry any angrier than he already is. Have you contacted Nate about this? Don't you think you should ask him to do it?"

Jake responded, "Nate is still overseas. Who knows when this world catastrophe is going to end? We need someone who is going to be with David daily. Besides, you're the one who helps Mom take care of the boys. It just makes sense."

"Okay, but what about Steven? Can't we have the court take Henry's rights to Steven away too?"

"It's a bit more complicated," her Uncle Robert answered. "We can't prove abuse in Steven's case."

Sarah looked at her uncles with pleading eyes. "You have to promise me you won't let Henry take Steven. I mean it. I need you to promise…"

Eddie was the first to respond. "Let us do the worrying, Sarah. We'll deal with Henry. Let him get upset. I've been waiting to bop him in the kisser for years. Maybe now I'll get my chance."

"Eddie, vatch your mouth around Sarah," Bubbe scolded. "Ve have to do something, Sarah. Henry is not fit to be a parent. Sarah, I don't vant you to vorry. Your uncles and I vill handle it."

Sarah soon found out what they meant by "handle it." Bubbe and her uncles hired an attorney, a friend of Louie's business partner. It was 1945, and taking custody of a child away from a parent, even an abusive one, was unheard of.

Finding out the family wanted her to be co-guardian with Bubbe was unnerving. She was only a kid herself. She couldn't take care of anyone else. Worse yet, she had been sworn to secrecy by her uncles and Bubbe. She couldn't even tell Mitzi. *What a mess!*

***

It would be several months before their case was heard in Family Court. Henry was notified by mail but didn't bother showing up. He did, however, call Bubbe a few hours before the hearing.

"Allo," Bubbe said, answering the phone.

"Molly, I'd better win the case, or you'll be sorry." Click.

Bubbe didn't know what to make of Henry's threat, but she wasn't going to back down, not this time.

The judge asked Sarah and Bubbe to testify. He reviewed the affidavits from family members and the hospital records and asked them to return the following day. Sarah prayed longer and harder that night than she ever had before. "Please, HaShem, I know I've asked you for a lot over the years, but this time, I truly need you on my side. Please don't let Henry hurt David again. Please."

The next morning, as the judge read his decision, Sarah knew her prayers had been answered. The court revoked Henry's parental rights over David and named Sarah and Bubbe co-guardians. To mark the occasion, Bubbe cooked everyone's favorite dishes. Together as a family, they celebrated Henry being out of their lives once and for all. Sarah began writing a rather lengthy letter to Nate, to keep him updated on the family happenings. But no one, not even Sarah, could have guessed what would happen next.

CHAPTER 7

Steven's Gone

I t had been several weeks since the guardianship decision, and things seemed to be settling down in the Steinman/Roth household. Encouraged by Bubbe, Sarah started attending the Future Bookkeepers after-school club meetings again. During the meeting, one afternoon, the school secretary knocked on the door and told Sarah there was a call for her in the main office. When she picked up the phone receiver, she immediately knew something was wrong. It wasn't only the tone of Bubbe's voice; her grandmother would never call the school unless someone was sick or had died.

"Bubbe, are you okay? Are the boys okay? Did someone get hurt?"

"Sarah, Sarah. Oh my lord, vhat have I done? Vill you ever forgive me?"

"Bubbe, what are you talking about? I love you. Take it easy and tell me what happened."

"Sarah, that horrible, vile man took Steven. He took our baby avay."

"Steven? Who took Steven? Henry?!"

"Yes, Henry." Bubbe went on to tell Sarah how Henry came by the house and instructed Steven to pack some clothes and leave everything else. Steven was shaking and crying. Henry told Bubbe he was taking his youngest son with him as repayment for Bubbe and Sarah taking custody of David away from him.

"He said, I stole you and David from him, but he vasn't going to let me keep Steven. He's taken him to Vashington, D.C. or Lord knows vhere."

At the end of the conversation, Sarah and Bubbe were both in tears. Sarah couldn't believe Henry had taken Steven. He didn't want him any more than he wanted Nate, Sarah, or David. He was getting even. Henry may have been Steven's legal guardian, but he never was a father in the true sense of the word.

Within weeks, Sarah began receiving letters from her grandfather, Sam, Henry's father, telling her Henry was beating Steven. Sam may not have approved of what his son was doing to his grandson, but he had created Henry in his own image.

Sarah remembered a time, soon after her mother died, she had been visiting with Sam and her grandmother, Clara. It was in the spring, and Sam was in the backyard, hard at work, digging a hole. At first, Sarah thought he was going to plant some flower bulbs. But as the hole grew larger, she wondered what he was going to put in the ground that needed such a large and deep space. After a few hours, her grandfather came into the house, sat down at the kitchen table, and announced to her grandmother that he had dug her grave, and now all she had to do was jump into it. They had been fighting earlier in the day, but then again, they were always fighting. Her grandmother began to cry. The expression on her grandfather's face had terrified Sarah to such a degree that she slept on the floor on her grandmother's side of the bed for the next few nights to make sure nothing happened to her.

Sarah was heartsick to hear that Henry was now abusing Steven. For years, she had made it her crusade to protect Steven from Henry's temper, and now she was unable to fulfill that promise. Henry wouldn't take any phone calls or answer any of the letters Sarah sent. With Steven gone, a part of her was missing.

Thinking back on her separation from Steven gave Sarah pause. How did she survive the last couple of years? Just like she survived her mother's death, she supposed, by putting it out of her mind. But none of that mattered now. Steven was safe and sound at home, and Henry was finally out of their lives. At least she hoped he was, but nothing was ever certain with Henry.

The morning after Steven's homecoming, Sarah returned to work. It would have been ideal if she could have taken the day off, but things were too hectic at the office. Bubbe had to push her out the door. "Go, Sarah. Steven vill be fine. Ve'll celebrate this veekend. Now, go-go-go!"

On her way to the bus stop, Sarah couldn't help thinking about her brother Nate. It had been so difficult during the war when he was away from them, and it made her realize how much she needed his counsel during those tumultuous times. She was glad that he had returned home safe and sound. Nate was one of three people in Sarah's life, besides Bubbe and Mitzi, who she could confide in.

Approaching the bus stop, Sarah noticed the 645 rounding the corner with her favorite driver, Charlie, at the wheel. After finding a window seat, not an easy feat in the mornings, she knew it was going to be a terrific day.

At the next stop, a woman, who appeared to be in her late fifties, sat down next to Sarah and smiled. Sarah loved meeting people on the bus.

"Hi, I'm Sarah," she said, turning toward the woman.

The woman nodded. "I'm Lenore. Pleased to make your acquaintance."

Sarah couldn't help but notice that Lenore had her salt and pepper hair pulled back with a headband, exposing her face, which didn't appear to have any makeup on it. Sarah thought it odd that anyone would go to work without at least wearing some blush or lipstick.

"What do you do, Lenore?" Sarah wondered what job she might have that allowed her to dress so casually.

"I work for a manufacturer as a bookkeeper."

That explained her plain appearance. She probably worked in a plant office, so a dress code didn't matter as much.

"That's such a coincidence," said Sarah. "I'm a bookkeeper too." During the bus ride, Sarah found out that Lenore helped raise her younger brothers and sisters. Sarah felt an immediate kinship with her.

Robin L.R. Kellogg

"Do you…if this is too personal, let me know…but do you have a boyfriend, Sarah?" Lenore asked.

"You can ask. You know how it is. I've dated a few boys but nothing serious. I'm too busy with my brothers right now to have a boyfriend." Lenore's eyes crinkled, and her smile dissolved.

"Sarah, if you don't mind me saying so, and I don't want to be rude, but don't sacrifice your life for your siblings. I think it's lovely that you are taking care of your family, but take it from someone who walked in those very shoes, make a life for yourself as well."

Before Sarah had a chance to say anything, Lenore continued, "I had the same attitude as you. I wanted to help my siblings, and I felt a responsibility to take care of them. I didn't date. One by one, they got married and had families of their own. They continued on with their lives. By the time everyone was grown, I was too old and set in my ways for a relationship. As much as I enjoy my nieces and nephews, I feel as if I cheated myself. Do yourself a favor and start living a little more for you."

Sarah wasn't sure what to say to Lenore. Before she knew it, Charlie had reached her stop. She thanked Lenore for the advice and wished her a good day, adding that she hoped they ran into one another again. She would have to think about what Lenore had told her but not now. Her focus was on celebrating Steven's return home.

Upon entering the office, Sarah saw that Rita was already at her desk. "Good morning, Rita. How are you on this beautiful day?"

Rita turned her body around, looking a bit bewildered. "You look like Sarah, but you don't sound like her. Who are you, and what have you done to my sweet, sad Sarah?"

"Very funny, Rita. Yesterday, a miracle happened. One that I thought would never occur!"

Rita searched Sarah's face to determine if she was joking or not. She seemed serious. "What happened?"

"Steven came home," Sarah said, beaming.

"You mean Steven, the brother who your father took with him to live in D.C.? That Steven?"

"Yes, can you believe it? The jerk got tired of him and sent him home."

24

"When did you find out?" asked Rita. "Yesterday when I received the telegram."

"Why didn't you tell me it was from your father?"

"I was too emotional and didn't want to start crying in the office. Besides, I didn't want to bother you or Mr. Thomas with my personal problems."

"I'm so happy for you and your family, Sarah. If you need any clothes for Steven, my Jeffrey is the same age. Some of his things might fit Steven. Just let me know."

"That's so sweet of you, Rita! Okay, I have to get to work on the accounts for Mr. Thomas. Talk to you later." Sarah sat down at her desk and started to review the data from the Zimmerman account that she had entered into the ledger the day before. As she continued to work on the books, she noticed something was off. The columns weren't adding up. She turned to ask Rita about it but noticed her officemate was in the middle of a phone conversation. It seemed private. She was whispering, and Sarah didn't want to disturb her. She'd ask her about it later. When Sarah looked up, she saw Mr. Thomas standing at her desk.

"I wanted to check with you about the Zimmerman account. How's it coming along? Do you think I'll have the general ledger numbers by the end of the day?"

"I was about to stop by your office, Mr. Thomas. I've noticed some inconsistencies and was hoping you could review my calculations. I know you told me to focus on the last two quarters, but I took the liberty of going back, and these inconsistencies seem to go on for at least a year, if not longer. It's odd. I could be totally off here, Mr. Thomas, but it looks like someone may be siphoning money from Mr. Zimmerman's business."

"That's absurd, Sarah," laughed Mr. Thomas. "Let me review it in my office. In the meantime, recalculate the numbers on paper, and I'll use the adding machine. Let's see if, between the two of us, we can't get to the bottom of this. Oh, and when Rita gets off the phone, ask her to help. You know she worked on this account until recently."

"Thanks, Mr. Thomas."

After recalculating the numbers again, Sarah peered at Mr. Thomas who was ensconced in his office, punching the keys on his adding machine. As if he knew she was watching him, Mr. Thomas got up from his desk and stuck his head out through his partially closed office door.

"Sarah, please get Mr. Zimmerman on the line for me."

Once she transferred the call, Mr. Thomas got up from his chair and shut the door to his office. She could only hear murmurs, but it sounded as if he was frustrated. Before Sarah left that day, Mr. Thomas came out of his office, looking as if he was ill. "I'm going home, Sarah. I've asked Rita to lock up."

"Sure thing, Mr. Thomas. I hope you feel better. See you tomorrow."

CHAPTER 8

Steven's Story

Bubbe was right. She said if Sarah gave Steven time, he would talk about his time with Henry.

One Sunday afternoon, Sarah and Steven were home alone. Bubbe was out visiting Uncle Jake and Aunt Rose. David was at a friend's house, and Nate was helping a friend work on his car.

Sarah was sitting in her grandmother's armchair, had snuggled under a blanket, and was prepared for a quiet afternoon reading, Wuthering Heights. It was a book Mitzi had loaned her. It took her awhile to get into the story, but once she did, she couldn't put it down. Poor Heathcliff. Hindley is just awful to him. But his romance with Catherine was...

"Sarah, are you busy right now?"

Peering over the top of her book, she saw Steven standing inches from her face.

"Steven, you see me, I'm reading now." Sarah rarely had a chance to sit down and relax, and she wasn't willing to give up her peace and quiet so easily.

"Well, how's the book so far?"

Sarah could see her chances of reading any further were diminishing.

"I feel like you have something on your mind. What is going on, Steven?"

"I keep thinking about when I was away. Sometimes, I still have nightmares about it."

"Oh." Sarah honestly didn't know what to say. Now he had her full attention. "Well, I'm a good listener. I'll tell you what. You talk, and I'll listen."

"Okay. You know, some nights I lay in bed and listen to the sirens from the police cars, and I start to shake and get all sweaty. The sirens remind me of living with Dad."

Dad. That's a word Sarah hadn't associated with Henry for a very long time.

"Lots of times either Dad's wife, Barbara, or Grandpa Sam would call the police. Barbara and Dad were always screaming at one another. I don't think they like each other very much. When the fighting started, I would sneak out through the kitchen door and wait in the alleyway. I don't even think they noticed I had left the house. You know Dad gets scary when he's angry. Anyway, I would hide there until the police were gone. I was afraid they would take me away from Dad and that I'd never see you guys again.

Sometimes I would talk to HaShem. I'd make deals with him, you know, like if you bring me back home, I'll be a good boy, and I won't cause anyone trouble."

Sarah could feel her eyes welling up with tears. *Steven blamed himself? How could he even think that?*

"Dad just didn't fight with Barbara. He fought with Grandma Clara and Grandpa Sam. He would say such mean things to Grandma. She was always so nice to me. She'd make me chicken soup with dumplings and her potato pancakes. She was the only one who ever hugged me. She would tell me that everything was going to be all right. I never believed her, but I don't think she knew what to say to me when Dad would hit me. I hated him when he did that. Did he ever hit you, Sarah?"

A wave of nausea overwhelmed Sarah, and she bolted for the bathroom.

"Sarah, are you okay? Are you sick?"

She was sick, sick to her stomach that Henry had touched Steven. This was a confirmation of what her Grandfather Sam had told her. She had been able to protect Steven before Henry took him to D.C., but there was nothing she could have done to prevent the damage caused over the last two years.

"Ugh, I'm fine, Steven. I think I may just have eaten some bad cheese. Let's sit down again so you can tell me more about your time with Henry. You mentioned you had fun with Grandma. What were some of the things you enjoyed doing with her?"

"Oh, that's easy. I loved helping her cook. She was happiest when she was cooking or baking. I think it might have been because it meant she didn't have to talk to Grandpa Sam or Dad. Grandpa Sam is mean like Dad sometimes. He screams and yells a lot and says horrible things to Grandma. When we cooked together, Grandma would always tell me stories about when she was a little girl in Poland and what it was like coming to America. On Sunday nights, we would listen to the radio. There was a show she loved about a judge and the cases he decided on."

Sarah was curious now. When she visited her grandparents in the past, Henry's mother was always so quiet and meek, as if it was her task in life to blend into the background and not to breathe too loud. She didn't remember her as animated as Steven was describing. This was another side of her Grandmother Clara that Sarah hadn't seen. "So, what was so special about listening to the show?"

"The best part was at the end of the show. The judge would say 'Good night, America' and Grandma would talk to the radio and say, 'Goodnight to you, Judge.' It was just funny how she talked to the radio as if the person playing the judge could hear her."

"That's not so odd, Steven. You and David always shout at the radio when a baseball game is on."

"That's different, Sarah!"

With her hand on her chest, Sarah said, "Oh, I guess you're right. The guys on the team are speaking directly to you and David. How silly of me!"

Steven rolled his eyes. "You're always so dramatic. No wonder why you don't have a boyfriend."

"Steven! I am not dramatic. I'm just pointing out that you do the same thing. And I don't have problems finding someone to date. Maybe I haven't found the right guy yet, or maybe I have, but that's none of your business."

Nate opened the door at that very moment. "The right guy, huh? You know you could meet my friend from work. He's seen your picture, and he thinks you're really pretty. He's Jewish, and he's a nice guy with a decent job. What else could you ask for?"

"Enough already! As I was telling Steven before you so rudely interrupted us, I am perfectly fine at the moment. And even if I wasn't, I certainly don't require any assistance from either of you!"

Nate turned his attention to Steven. "Hey, buddy. How are you holding up? I see you had to spend the afternoon with our sister who apparently took a grouchy pill today."

"I'm fine. I was just telling Sarah about when I lived with Dad. She told me to talk, and she would listen. And she kept her word too."

"Wow, Sarah. I'm impressed. Not a word, huh?"

Before she even had a chance to respond to Nate's comment, Steven jumped in.

"Oh, and one more thing, Nate. Don't eat the cheese! It got Sarah sick, and she had to throw up right in the middle of my story. I've never had anyone do that before."

CHAPTER 9

Missing in Action

M r. Thomas was holed up in his office for the next couple days and was refusing all calls—even from Mr. Zimmerman. He wouldn't even speak with Sarah, other than to tell her not to disturb him.

"I hope Mr. Thomas is okay. Has he spoken to you, Rita?"

"Nope; he sure hasn't. It's very odd. For all the years I've worked for Mr. Thomas, I've never known him to stay mum for this long."

Mr. Zimmerman called the office several times, asking to speak with Mr. Thomas. Upon hearing he wasn't available on the fourth attempted call, Mr. Zimmerman began shouting at Sarah. "You tell your boss I want my calls returned. I will not be ignored!" Then he slammed down the receiver, startling Sarah. She had a feeling that Mr. Thomas was avoiding Mr. Zimmerman's calls because he felt so foolish for not identifying the missing funds sooner. Her boss was such a nice man, and he believed in giving his employees latitude so they would take greater pride in their work. Sarah was near tears as she got off the phone. She hated it when people yelled; it reminded her of Henry. "Are you okay, honey?" Rita asked.

"Mr. Zimmerman is so upset," Sarah sniffed. "I don't know what to tell him. I…"

"Hey, Sarah, why don't you and I take a break? Let's sit down and have some tea? It will calm your nerves."

As Rita made tea, Sarah slowly became more composed. Handing her a teacup, Rita said, "Now, honey, why don't you tell me why you're so upset."

Sarah filled Rita in on the deficits in the Zimmerman account and told her how Mr. Thomas was acting so strangely. She wondered if the inconsistencies in the Zimmerman books were the only reason he had become so reclusive.

"You don't think Mr. Thomas had anything to do with this mess, do you, Rita? He's such a nice man, and I enjoy working for him. I'm just concerned for him. I hope he doesn't blame me for any of this."

"I'm sure it will all work itself out, Sarah. I don't know if Mr. Thomas is responsible for any of this or not, but he'll know what to do to fix it. Don't worry about your job. Mr. Thomas is happy with your performance. I'm sure he doesn't blame you for any of this," Rita said, trying to comfort her.

"I hope you're right about that, Rita."

***

Following dinner that night, Bubbe noticed Sarah wasn't her usual self and was moping around the apartment. "Sveetheart, you look so sad, like you lost your best friend. Is there anything I can do?"

"Something's odd with Mr. Thomas. He hasn't been the same since speaking with Mr. Zimmerman a few days ago. Something's wrong. I know it."

"Oh, Sarah, alvays taking the veight of the vorld on your shoulders. I'm sure Mr. Thomas is fine."

Sarah wanted to believe Bubbe, but her gut was telling her that something was wrong, and right now, she was more inclined to listen to her gut.

CHAPTER 10

Early Morning Meeting

It had been over a week since Mr. Thomas had the hush-hush conversations with Mr. Zimmerman. Sarah feared something was terribly wrong and decided she would grill Rita about it when she got to the office.

As she walked in, Sarah found Rita staring intently at a letter in her typewriter.

"Good morning, Rita."

Rita didn't respond.

Sarah, who thought it best not to disturb her, sat down at her desk, and took out her general ledger. It wasn't until Sarah pushed against the back of her chair and it creaked that Rita moved.

"Sarah, you're here. I didn't even hear you come in. Sorry, sweetie, Mr. Thomas called me at home last night, asking me to come in early. He said he and Mr. Zimmerman were going to speak by phone, and he wanted me to be here to field the other phone calls. Now, don't be upset, Sarah. He was going to contact you, but I told him that you were having family issues. I suppose he didn't want to bother you."

"Rita, you shouldn't have told him that. I don't want Mr. Thomas to feel like I can't handle the job because I can."

"He knows that, Sarah. He needed one of us here, and when I said I could be in early, he left it at that. Don't get yourself all worked up. It's not a big deal."

The phone at Rita's desk rang. "Yes, Mr. Thomas, I'll make sure to tell you when Mr. Zimmerman calls."

Turning back toward Sarah, she said, "Hon, I have to run to the powder room. If my phone rings, can you answer it? It may be Mr. Zimmerman."

"Okay, but why is Mr. Zimmerman calling your number? I'm Mr. Thomas's assistant."

"Mr. Thomas has asked Mr. Zimmerman to contact me directly. Now, don't read anything into this. I think he feels confident that I can handle Mr. Zimmerman when he's, shall we say, cantankerous."

Just at that moment, Mr. Thomas came out of his office. "Good morning, Sarah. When you have time, come into my office. I have some client files I need to discuss with you."

"Sure thing, Mr. Thomas."

Sarah finished what she was doing and went into her boss's office. Mr. Thomas gave her instructions on the client files. "I think that's it, Sarah, thank you."

Heading toward the door, she stopped in her tracks. "Mr. Thomas, are you upset with me? Did I do anything wrong? I feel as if I opened up a can of worms by telling you what I found in the Zimmerman file."

"Upset with you? No, not at all, Sarah. You were right on the money with your numbers. Zimmerman and I are just trying to fig-ure out who is finagling the account. Nothing for you to be con-cerned with. Now if you don't mind, I need to make a few phone calls."

"Sure, Mr. Thomas. I'll close the door on my way out." Walking back to her desk, Sarah had an uneasy feeling in her stomach that something was going on, and no one was letting her in on the secret. Later, upon returning from lunch, Sarah saw Mr. Zimmerman sit-ting in Mr. Thomas's office. "Rita, did you know Mr. Zimmerman was coming in?"

"No, he had mentioned to Mr. Thomas that he might come by, but he never confirmed it."

"Don't you find it odd that he didn't make an appointment?" asked Sarah.

"Mr. Zimmerman is a very nice man," Rita said lowering her voice, "but he likes to keep people guessing. It's not at all unlike him to stop by unannounced."

Looking toward Mr. Thomas's office, Sarah caught Mr. Zimmerman's eye. They had never met before and had only spoken on the telephone a few times. Oh no, Mr. Zimmerman was leaving Mr. Thomas's office and walking directly toward her.

"Miss Sarah Steinman, I presume?"

"Y-y-e-ss, that's me," she said, extending her hand.

Mr. Zimmerman took her hand up to his lips, kissing it lightly. "You, my dear, are a lifesaver."

CHAPTER 11

Thank You

The next morning, Sarah received a breathtaking bouquet of lilies, her favorite flower. The card read, "Dear Miss Steinman, you'll never know what your dedication means to me." It was signed, Mr. Zimmerman.

Now Sarah was truly confused. If Mr. Zimmerman was initially so upset with Mr. Thomas, then why was he so happy with Sarah? Before she had a chance to give it much thought, Sarah caught sight of the most handsome young man she had ever seen, heading for her boss's office. He winked at Rita as he passed by her desk. Sarah was mesmerized by his presence. He had medium-brown curly hair, an olive complexion, and striking dark-brown eyes set into a perfectly oval face. He was well-built and dressed to the nines. She wondered what his name was.

Feeling a tap on her shoulder, she turned around to find Rita smirking at her with that all-knowing motherly look. "Sarah, that's Jonathan Silver, Mr. Zimmerman's nephew. Mr. Zimmerman has been grooming him to take over his clothing business. You can stop staring at him now."

"Oh, I wasn't looking at him. I barely noticed that he walked into the office," she said, turning back to the work on her desk.

"Sure, you didn't," Rita said.

Within an hour of his arrival, the young Mr. Silver was taking his leave. He greeted Rita with a hug. Sarah saw them talking and noticed Rita pointing toward her. *Oh no, she wouldn't. How could she? I'm so embarrassed. I could just die.*

"Sarah Steinman?" "Yes, I'm Sarah."

"I'm Jonathan Silver," he said, extending his hand. "My uncle, Mr. Zimmerman, told me how you found a glitch in his accounts payable. He's eternally grateful."

"Glad to hear it, but I was just doing my job. Have you worked with your uncle long?"

"A few years now, but it's much too long a story to tell you while we stand here. Do you take a lunch hour?"

"I do, but I can't," Sarah sputtered.

"Can't what?"

"Go with you to lunch. I don't date much."

"Who said anything about a date? I'm asking you out for a business lunch. I want to get to know my uncle's new hero."

Remembering that Lenore had advised her to live a little, Sarah answered, "Okay, but it has to be kosher."

"What has to be kosher?" Jonathan asked.

"The place we choose for lunch, silly. There's Benny's Deli right down the street, that is, if it's okay with you," said Sarah.

"Benny's it is. I'll pick you up at noon tomorrow."

After he had left the office, Sarah dashed over to Rita's desk to find out anything she could about her new mystery man. Rita told her he was twenty-six, the only son of Mr. Zimmerman's sister, Evelyn. He had grown up in Paterson, New Jersey, just a few towns away, and had graduated from New York University.

As Rita went on to give her other details about Jonathan's life, Sarah's head was spinning. *Maybe Lenore was right after all. It was exciting to have something of her own to look forward to.*

CHAPTER 12

Mr. Dreamboat

J ust as he had promised, Jonathan came by the office a few minutes before noon and whisked Sarah off to lunch at Benny's down the street. She couldn't stop laughing during lunch as Jonathan regaled her with stories about his childhood.

"You have a beautiful smile, Sarah. What do you say we go out on Saturday night?"

"For a date?"

"Yes, for a date, Sarah."

"I'd love to but…"

"What?"

"You're going to think I'm crazy."

"Sarah, nothing you could say would make me think you're crazy. What is it?"

"Well, I live with my grandmother, and she'll expect to meet you before you take me out on a date."

"I can come over earlier on Saturday."

"No, it will still be Shabbas. Maybe we can go out on Sunday? And you can stop by a little early and meet her?"

"It's a date," said Jonathan, "but you have to promise me one thing."

"What's that?"

"That you'll smile a lot. You're so beautiful when you smile."

Sarah was smitten. She had never had such a handsome man take interest in her. Arriving home that evening, she told her grandmother about her upcoming date with Mr. Zimmerman's nephew, Jonathan. "Bubbe, he's Jewish, he's handsome, and he's so sophisticated."

"Sarah, I'm thrilled for you, mamala. I vant to know more about him before you go out on your date."

"That's the best part, Bubbe. He's stopping by Sunday before we go out so you can meet him."

Bubbe smiled and hoped that she was able to be a little more discerning with this young man than she had been with Henry when he first showed up. She was not going to allow history to repeat itself. Not on her watch.

Sarah had arranged with Jonathan to stop by at 1:00 p.m. on Sunday. That would give Bubbe time to ask her questions and still allow Jonathan and Sarah a few hours to spend together.

To keep the boys from poking their noses into the conversation, she convinced Uncle Louie to take them to the park.

A few minutes before 1:00 p.m., Sarah heard a knock at the front door and rushed out of her bedroom where she had been getting ready for the past hour. "I'm coming," she yelled as she raced to open it. There was Jonathan dressed in a pair of black slacks, a starched white shirt, and a gray-and-white herringbone sports jacket. He was holding a bouquet of lilies in his hand. He looked heavenly.

"These are for you, Sarah," said Jonathan as he handed the flowers to her.

"Sarah, vhy don't we put those in vater," said Bubbe who was standing behind her. Sticking her hand out, Bubbe introduced herself to Jonathan.

"Hi, I'm Molly Roth, Sarah's grandmother."

"Yes, ma'am. It's lovely to meet you. You have a beautiful granddaughter. I can see she takes after her grandmother. Sarah said you wanted to meet me. What do you want to know? I'm an open book."

Molly didn't know how to respond. A feeling of unease surrounded her as if he was anything but an open book. The last time she felt this way was when Rose introduced her to Henry years ago.

"Vell, come in, sit, sit," said Bubbe, leading him over to the couch. "You vant a bisl tea? Some babka?"

Sarah could tell by Jonathan's confused look that he had no idea what Bubbe just asked him.

"She asked you if you want a little tea and cake?"

"Yes, ma'am."

"Good, good. I'll put a kettle on. Then ve'll talk. Sarah, come help me in the kitchen."

"Sure, Bubbe. I'll be just a few minutes, Jonathan."

Once in the kitchen, Sarah saw her grandmother had a look of concern on her face. "Bubbe," she whispered. "What's wrong?"

"Sarah, he's a very handsome young man and so polite. Maybe a little too polite? Vhat do you know about him? Are you sure he's Jewish? Doesn't he speak Yiddish? Vhat kind of family does he come from? I just, he just…"

"He just what, Bubbe?"

"He reminds me of Henry." There, she had said it.

"He's nothing like my father!" said Sarah, trying to keep her voice down. She didn't want Jonathan to overhear the conversation.

"I just vant you to be safe."

"Bubbe, please, I really like him. Please give him a chance. Okay?"

"Shah," her grandmother said softly. Shah could mean anything from shush to a sterner be quiet, but Sarah knew from her grandmother's tone that the former applied.

"The tea's ready, and ve don't want to keep your young man vaiting," Bubbe said as she poured the tea into glasses and asked Sarah to bring it into the living room. Sarah was surprised to see Jonathan sitting in Bubbe's club chair, surveying the room. The intensity of his gaze gave Sarah pause. Something about it was all too familiar. On second thought, it was probably nothing. She was a bit rattled from her talk with Bubbe.

For the next hour, Bubbe riddled the conversation with questions about Jonathan's family and his plans for the future. She ended with, "Jonathan, Sarah is my heart. I vant you to treasure her as if she vere the most valuable thing in the vorld because she is to our family."

Sarah turned red and wondered why Bubbe felt it necessary to say this to Jonathan. On their way out the door, Bubbe shook Jonathan's hand and took Sarah's face in her hands. Kissing her cheek, she quietly said in her ear, "Mamala, he seems like a nice young man. Have a good time."

Once the door closed, Molly sighed, knowing she didn't believe a word she had just said to her granddaughter.

That afternoon, Jonathan and Sarah went to the Capital Theater in downtown Passaic to see The Secret Life of Walter Mitty, about a man who overcame a less than fulfilling life by living in a dreamworld. When the lights went out, Jonathan put his arm around Sarah's shoulders. It remained there for the entire film.

If it had been anyone else, she would have removed their arm, as any proper young lady should, but she felt safe with Jonathan. I could get used to this, she thought. He continued to fuss over her at dinner, making sure that it was a perfect evening.

When Sarah returned home, hours later, she looked as if she'd had the time of her life. She couldn't stop talking about how wonderful Jonathan was and how they were going out again the following weekend.

After Sarah had retired for the evening, Molly sat in her armchair, going over the conversation she had just had with her granddaughter. *Am I questioning Jonathan's character because I'm scared that history will repeat itself, or am I seeing him for what he is, a carbon copy of Henry?* she wondered.

***

The next morning, Sarah wore a smile that could light the world up. Molly knew her granddaughter's upbeat mood had everything to do with that young man she was so smitten with. He certainly put on a good show, but Bubbe didn't trust him as far as she could throw him, and that wasn't very far at all. However, she realized that sharing her suspicions with Sarah, about Jonathan, would only fall on deaf ears. Or if Sarah was anything like her mother, it would drive her right into his arms. She decided to keep her thoughts to herself.

Arriving at work that morning, Sarah raced over to Rita's desk to give her a full report on how dreamy her date with Jonathan had been.

"Okay, okay, so he's smart, sexy, and not too bad to look at," said Rita. "Doesn't he have any downfalls?"

"None," said Sarah, hugging herself. "Not one single thing."

Yep, Rita thought, Sarah is definitely stuck on him.

CHAPTER 13

Uncle Leonard and Aunt Becky

Mr. Thomas seemed to have reverted back to his old congenial self again. This certainly helped lessen Sarah's anxiety levels and made work fun again. While Mr. Zimmerman was visiting the office, one afternoon, he stopped by Sarah's desk to chat.

"Well, Sarah, I hear you're keeping my nephew out of trouble."

"I'm not sure that I'm keeping him out of trouble, but he is very sweet, and I enjoy spending time with him."

"Good. Good. I'd like to invite you to join Jonathan at my home for dinner next Sunday. I've already told him I was going to ask you. Can you make it?

"Oh, sir, that's so kind of you. Yes, I'll be there."

"I'll expect you on Sunday then. Unfortunately, my sister, Evelyn, Jonathan's mother, won't be able to join us, but she sends her regards."

That Sunday evening, as Jonathan drove his navy and tan Pontiac around to the far end of the circular driveway at his aunt and uncle's home, Sarah was in awe. Mr. Zimmerman had a palatial Victorian-style house. The stately home featured several steeped roofs and turrets and a large wraparound porch. As they got closer, Sarah could see a gazebo off to the far right, which led to beautiful gardens. A large bay window near the front door was flanked by two stained glass windows. Sarah couldn't make the pattern out at first, but as they got closer to the home, she saw it more clearly. It was a bouquet of lilies with white, yellow, and purple flowers, Sarah's favorite. It was breathtaking.

As they approached the home's large wooden double doors, she wondered what it would be like to live in such a house.

Jonathan interrupted her thoughts when he gave her a peck on the cheek. "Hey, Sarah, Sarah?"

"Oh, sorry. I just was thinking…"

His aunt and uncle answered the door together. Sarah was so overwhelmed by the size of the home that she stood there, unable to utter a word.

"Sarah, I'd like you to meet my Aunt Becky, and you already know my Uncle Leonard, of course."

Sarah had never thought to ask what Mr. Zimmerman's first name was. Leonard didn't quite suit him. He seemed much too personable to be a Leonard. Mrs. Zimmerman was beautiful. She had auburn hair and green eyes. Sarah couldn't stop staring at her.

"She's so excited to meet you," Sarah heard Jonathan say to his aunt. "I think she's just nervous."

"Sorry," interjected Sarah. "I'm admiring your beautiful home. I've never seen anything like it."

"Nothing to worry about, sweetheart," said Aunt Becky. "Let's sit down in the library. It's the first door on your right. Leonard, would you mind getting us some beverages from the kitchen? It's all set up on the tray."

"Duty calls," laughed Mr. Zimmerman. "I'll be right with you."

Sarah nodded to Mr. Zimmerman. As they walked toward the library, Sarah was intent on memorizing every inch of the home so that she could describe it to Bubbe once she returned home that evening. From its beautiful wall coverings and chandeliers, which adorned the foyer and the hallway, to the richness of the library, with its mahogany walls and built-in bookcases. Some of the shelves were open and others enclosed by glass doors, and there was also a large round table with a scalloped top, inset with tooled leather.

"Please sit," Aunt Becky said, pointing to a large, overstuffed couch while she took a seat in the club chair facing the pair. "I'd like to learn a bit more about the young woman who has captivated Jonathan's attention. Sarah, tell me a little bit about yourself and your family."

"Don't start your story without me," said Mr. Zimmerman, entering the room with a tray full of saucers and cups and a matching teapot. After placing the tray on the coffee table, he sat in the armchair near his wife. "Okay, go on."

"Well, I live with my grandmother and three brothers," Sarah began. She went on to tell them about her aunts and uncles and how wonderful they had been to her and her siblings. Sarah purposely left Henry out of the conversation. No need to bring him up. It would just put a damper on the evening, and she was so enjoying herself. "Oh, and I love working for Mr. Thomas."

"Yes, speaking of that," said Mr. Zimmerman, "I never properly thanked you for detecting the missing funds in my accounts. I can't tell you how appreciative I am. I'd like to do something special for you, Sarah."

Sarah's heart was beating faster than it had ever beat before.

"I'd like to offer you a job at my company," said Mr. Zimmerman.

"What would I do?" asked Sarah.

"The same work you do for Roy Thomas. I need someone sharp and detail-oriented like you on my team. As time goes on, if you're agreeable, I will train you to be a manager, like Jonathan is."

"I don't know what to say," answered Sarah. "Thank you. It's very generous of you!"

"Don't thank me. It was Jonathan's idea." Sarah looked toward Jonathan who gazed at her as if he were peering into her soul.

"I don't want you to rush with this decision. Take your time and think about it. Oh, and don't worry about Thomas. I'll work things out with him."

Sarah didn't know what to think. It was all too much to handle. On the way home that evening, Jonathan kept telling her how he hoped she would take the job because it meant they could spend more time together. Sarah agreed that it was a great opportunity but she felt torn, due to an allegiance she felt to Mr. Thomas. He was the one who had taken a chance on her when she had only been, a recent high school graduate with limited bookkeeping experience.

When she arrived home, Sarah sat down with Bubbe and told her everything about the Zimmermans' home and how special they had treated her. Molly listened intently. Since she hadn't officially accepted the job offer, Sarah decided not to tell her grandmother about it just yet. She wanted to call Mitzi to tell her about the date, the beautiful house, and more about Jonathan, but it was too late to phone her now. It would have to wait until tomorrow.

CHAPTER 14

Have You Decided Yet?

For the next week, Jonathan called Sarah daily to see if she could have lunch with him. Sarah thought it was sweet how he wanted to see her as much as he could. However, his favorite topic of conversation was becoming a bit tiresome.

"Have you decided to take my uncle up on his offer yet, Sarah?"

"Jonathan, you know this is a difficult decision. I want to make sure I do what's best. Please stop pressuring me." After speaking with Mitzi, she decided to feel things out before jumping feet first into the water. "I'm still thinking about it, Jonathan. I appreciate your uncle's offer, I do, but I enjoy working for Mr. Thomas. I feel as if I owe him my loyalty. He took a chance on me when no one else would. Oh, I don't think I mentioned it. Mr. Thomas gave your uncle's account back to me. Isn't that exciting?!"

In seconds, Jonathan's lips tightened, and his smile disappeared. "Why would that be such great news? Are you trying to tell me you're too good to work for my uncle?"

"No! Where did that come from? I only meant that it seems whatever caused the tension between Mr. Zimmerman and Mr. Thomas is over, and besides, I enjoy working on your uncle's books."

"I bet you just want to find a problem with them again," Jonathan said snidely.

"No, it's not that at all," Sarah blurted out, wondering why Jonathan was taking the conversation in this direction. "Look, Jonathan, I didn't mean to upset you. I don't want to fight. As I said, I'm still weighing your uncle's job offer."

"Well, he's not going to wait for your answer forever you know. He can hire anyone to be a bookkeeper!"

Although Sarah knew that to be true, hearing it from Jonathan still stung. Before she could say a word, Jonathan was back to his sweet old self again.

"Sorry if I upset you. I just want what's best for you, that's all. Let's get you back to the office before mean, old Mr. Thomas gets grumpy," he said with a smile.

Sarah tried to return his smile but just couldn't quite get the corners of her mouth to cooperate.

Upon her arrival home that evening, she wanted more than anything to tell Bubbe about what had happened with Jonathan, but knowing her grandmother's concerns about him, she thought it best to keep it to herself.

CHAPTER 15

A Betrayal of Trust

It had been a week since Mr. Zimmerman had first offered Sarah the job. Jonathan was still asking her why she wasn't jumping at the chance to work for his uncle, and Sarah was wondering why herself. Before she got too lost in her thoughts, her desk phone rang. It was Mr. Thomas's extension.

"Sarah, Mr. Zimmerman is due to be here in about half an hour. Can you get his file ready, and bring it into my office?"

"I'll do that right now, Mr. Thomas."

Sarah still hadn't told anyone about the job offer. No need to ruffle any feathers until she was sure which direction she wanted to take.

Mr. Zimmerman showed up an hour late for his appointment. On his way to Mr. Thomas's office, he glanced toward Sarah and winked. Sarah wasn't sure what the wink was all about, but after another fifteen minutes, Mr. Thomas and Mr. Zimmerman emerged from the office and headed toward her desk.

"Sarah, I hear Mr. Zimmerman has generously offered you a job, and I also understand that you've accepted it," said Mr. Thomas.

"I've...what? I don't know what to say..."

"Don't say a word, Sarah, although I wish you would have come and told me before Zimmerman here did. It took me a bit by surprise, but I understand why you would want to work there."

"Mr. Thomas, I am really sorry," she blurted out before being interrupted by Mr. Zimmerman.

"Sarah seems to be using messengers to get her news out. It wasn't until Jonathan told me she had accepted the position that I found out. In fact, I still haven't gotten confirmation from our girl here."

At this point, Sarah was in a tizzy. She couldn't decide what to do first: wring Jonathan's neck for assuming it was okay for him to speak for her, scream at Mr. Zimmerman for telling Mr. Thomas before he had even confirmed it with her, or crawl on her hands and knees and beg for Mr. Thomas's forgiveness. Instead, she began to cry, bawl to be more accurate. She couldn't stop the tears from coming, running from the office into the powder room to avoid having to look at either Mr. Zimmerman or Mr. Thomas. Once safely ensconced behind the locked door, she could breathe again. *Think, Sarah. Think. What am I going to do?*

"Sarah." It was Rita's voice.

Oh God. She couldn't face her, not now. Rita must think she was awful. Sarah heard a knocking at the door.

"Sarah. It's Rita. Why don't you come out so we can talk?" "You must think I'm ridiculous, don't you? I'm humiliated."

"Sarah, please just come out."

"O-kay. Only if you promise not to scold me."

"I promise."

Sarah opened the stall door, emerging with a puffy red face. Rita handed her some tissues.

"You didn't know Jonathan told his uncle you had accepted the job, did you?"

"No. I didn't. I told Jonathan that I was considering it. That I would think it over. That's all. I swear."

"Well, now that the cat's out of the bag, what are you going to do about it?"

"I don't know, Rita. I enjoy working here with you and Mr. Thomas. I also think I'm falling for Jonathan, but then he goes and does something like this, and I just don't know anymore."

Waiting for Sarah to return from the powder room, Leonard Zimmerman wondered aloud, "What in the world could have gotten Sarah so upset?"

"I don't know, Leonard. I've never seen her get so emotional. She's usually very levelheaded, even with her family situation."

"What do you mean, her family situation?"

"Sarah helps her grandmother and older brother raise her two younger brothers and has been doing so for the last few years."

"She's a bit young to have that kind of responsibility, isn't she?"

"Tell me about it. I've tried to be somewhat of a mentor to her because she is so young, and she doesn't really have anything of a parental figure in her life. Now I guess that'll be your job," he added, slapping his old friend on the back as he walked him to the door.

On his way back to the office, Leonard wondered if his nephew was mature enough to handle everything going on in Sarah's life. He'd have to keep an eye on them for both their sakes.

CHAPTER 16

The Reckoning

S arah left the powder room feeling a bit calmer but still quite angry with Jonathan. She decided being honest was the best policy. Walking toward Mr. Thomas she said, "Mr. Thomas, I want you to know that Jonathan spoke out of turn. It's true that Mr. Zimmerman offered me a position and that I promised to consider it. However, it is not true that I have made a final decision. I enjoy working with you and Rita. I can't tell you how much I appreciate your giving me this job and continuing to entrust me with more responsibilities. I think that's why I'm so torn. I would miss you and Rita terribly."

Mr. Thomas took her hands in his and with slightly watery eyes said, "My dear, you have a job here as long as you like. I would appreciate two weeks' notice if you decide to work for Leonard Zimmerman. And if you do leave and need a job recommendation in the future, know that I will always provide one to you. You have become like one of my family. I only want the best for you."

"Thank you, Mr. Thomas, thank you," Sarah said, her face beaming with relief.

At promptly 5:00 p.m. on the dot, Jonathan showed up at Thomas Finance for his dinner date with Sarah. Tapping the crystal on the face of his watch and grinning from ear to ear, he said, "It's quitting time. Time for fun and games with your guy!"

"At the moment, I'm not sure you are my guy. In fact, I'm not even sure I ever want to see you again," Sarah said as she took her purse out of the desk drawer and slammed it shut.

"I'm wounded," Jonathan said, holding a hand to his heart.

"You're wounded? You're wounded? We've got to talk, mister, and now."

"We've got to talk, mister, and now," Jonathan said in a deep, mocking voice. "Geez, Sarah, lighten up. What's gotten your knickers in a twist?"

"Let's go. There are things I need to say that just aren't appropriate for mixed company," she said, looking at Rita.

At dinner, Jonathan sat next to her. He reached for her hand, but Sarah wiggled her hand away. "You will not touch me until you've answered some questions."

"Okay, shoot."

"Don't give me any ideas," she said wryly. "Do you know what happened today? I'll tell you what happened! Your uncle came into the office and told Mr. Thomas that I had accepted his job offer. Now, here's the strange part. I don't remember ever telling him or you that I had made a final decision. Do you know the predicament you put me in? Do you understand the consequences of what you've done?" Sarah asked in utter exasperation.

Looking at her with a bemused expression, he answered, "You were taking far too long to decide to accept what is probably the best and only offer you'll receive right now. I was just moving things along at a more reasonable pace. You should be thanking me for taking the burden off you and not accusing me of taking liberties with your decisions."

Sarah couldn't believe her ears. The guy she thought was Mr. Dreamy just a day ago had turned into someone completely different. "Come on, baby doll. You're just mad that I leaked your news before you did. You know I would never do anything to harm you. I just can't wait until we're working side by side with one another."

"You may have to wait a bit longer. After your uncle left, I told Mr. Thomas that you spoke out of turn and that I hadn't made a final decision yet."

"You what?! Sarah, why would you do that? I set up the perfect scenario for you to leave that dead-end job, and you find a way to screw it up. Geez," he said, shaking his head.

"Jonathan, it's not a dead-end job." Sarah placed her napkin on her lap. Jonathan took the opportunity to insert his hand between her legs, slowly inching it up her thigh.

"Jonathan!" Sarah said as quietly as she could. Still whispering, she added, "What do you think you're doing?"

"I think I'm showing my girl how much I like her. Nothing wrong with that, is there?"

"There is, if I'm your girl," Sarah answered, pushing his hand away.

"Come on, Sarah. Don't act all prim and proper. Let a guy have some fun."

"I have nothing against you having fun. I have a problem with you touching me down there and doing it in public to boot."

"If it's being in public that bothers you, we can go to my car, baby, and I can…"

"No. You. Can't. Look, Jonathan, I know this may sound old-fashioned, but I'm a good girl. I promised my Bubbe that I wouldn't be intimate with anyone until I was married to them."

"Come on, Sarah, what your grandmother doesn't know won't hurt her," he said, once again moving his hand quite higher up her leg than she was comfortable with.

She had had enough. Sarah smacked his hand and stormed out of the restaurant. She always carried a few dollars with her, her mad money, just in case of an emergency. She would take the bus home.

Seated at the bus stop, Sarah watched as Jonathan pulled his Pontiac up to the curb. He stopped in front of her, leaning over to roll down the passenger window.

"Sarah, I'm sorry. I really am. Please get in the car."

"No."

"Come on, baby doll, get in the car."

"I'm taking the bus home, Jonathan."

"Dammit, Sarah. I said get in the car. Now!"

"No, and don't speak to me in that tone ever again," she said, beginning to feel very unsettled.

Jonathan glared at Sarah, pressed the gas, and sped off.

***

The next morning, when she arrived at work, there was an envelope on her desk.

"Where did this come from, Rita?"

Rita shrugged her shoulders and turned back to her filing. Opening it, Sarah saw it was from Jonathan. It read:

> Sarah, please forgive me. Don't allow our argument last night to destroy what could be a beautiful relationship.

If he thought a note was enough to excuse his behavior yesterday, he had another thing coming.

CHAPTER 17

An Uncomfortable Spot

Sarah had told Mr. Thomas she was going to contact Mr. Zimmerman and explain that Jonathan had accepted the job on her behalf, but after starting to dial the number a half dozen times, she lost her nerve, that is until her boss came by her desk, asking her if she had made the call yet.

"Not yet, Mr. Thomas. Mr. Zimmerman scares me just a little bit. I don't want him to bite my head off."

"Leonard has his moments, Sarah, but he's reasonable. Give him a call. I'm sure it will all turn out well."

After reaching out to Mr. Zimmerman, he told her that under the circumstances, he understood her wanting to think things through. However, he was convinced that Jonathan never meant to be controlling or make the decision for her, but rather that he only wanted the best for her.

"Can I get a final answer from you by the end of next week, Sarah?" asked Mr. Zimmerman.

"I can do that, sir. I'm sorry it's taken me so long. It's not every day that I have two companies vying for my services."

"I understand," he said with a laugh. "I await your decision, my dear."

Sarah was relieved that Mr. Thomas and Mr. Zimmerman both were privy to the situation that Jonathan had put her in. *Now, what to do about Jonathan?* His actions the other day were inexcusable, yet she liked him and didn't want to end the relationship because of a misunderstanding. Maybe Rita would have some insight into this.

Later in the afternoon, when things had calmed down a bit in the office, Sarah invited Rita for a cup of tea in the conference room.

"What's going on? asked Rita. "Were you able to square things away with Mr. Thomas and Mr. Zimmerman?"

"I think so, at least I hope so. I told them both that Jonathan had spoken out of turn and that I was considering the new position but hadn't made a final decision yet, one way or the other."

"Well, that's good. So why do you still look so sad?"

"Oh, Rita, it's Jonathan."

"Mr. Dreamboat?"

"Maybe not. I was hoping you could tell me if I overreacted."

"Sure. Shoot."

Sarah proceeded to fill Rita in on all details from the night before, including Jonathan's immature and angry behavior.

"He sounds a little immature, but aren't all men?" Rita tittered.

"I don't know. Something my grandmother said has been bothering me, and I just can't stop thinking about it."

"What did she say?"

"The first time she met Jonathan, she said he reminded her of…"

"Spit it out."

"Henry," said Sarah.

"Why would she say that? I mean, what exactly reminded her of your father?"

"She said he was very handsome, like Henry was at that age."

"Is that all?" asked Rita. "From the way you said it, I thought she pegged him as a nut."

"No, you don't understand. My grandmother may have said it was his looks, but it's what she didn't say that concerns me. She kept telling Jonathan how precious I was to the family as if she was afraid he was going to harm me."

"Sarah, there you go again, seeing innuendos when I'm sure none were intended. Molly's your grandmother. I'd expect her to be protective of you. Here's a thought. Why don't you give Jonathan a chance to redeem himself? If he messes up, then you'll know you were right, and then you can break it off."

"I don't know. Why is it so hard? I like him, and when he's in a good mood, he's sweet and kind, and he can't do enough for me. But he scared me last night."

"Why don't you tell him that he scared you? I'll bet that wasn't his intention."

Maybe Rita had a point. She would call Jonathan to see if they could meet for a heart-to-heart talk. Sarah had been so focused on Jonathan she almost forgot about getting her daily accounting reports to Mr. Thomas. *Yikes.* She needed to complete this before the end of the workday, but she found her concentration floundering. Her mind kept switching back to thoughts about Jonathan.

Sarah glanced at her wristwatch; it had belonged to her mother. The watch was one of the few things she had left from her. *Oh, dear.* It said 4:30 p.m. *How did it get so late?* She felt like she had just barely sat down when her phone rang.

"Good afternoon, Thomas Finance Company. How may I help you?"

"Sarah, it's Jonathan. Please…don't hang up. I know I acted like a jerk. I like you, and I don't want to mess this up. I know we haven't known each other for that long, but I think we have something pretty special going on here."

"Jonathan, look I…"

"Let me finish, Sarah. I've never met someone like you before. You balance me out. I feel complete when I'm with you."

Sarah wasn't sure how to respond but knew she had a lot to get off her chest. It was just a matter of getting her vocal cords to cooperate. She desperately wanted to believe that he was sincere, but she couldn't get her grandmother's voice out of her head.

"Sarah? Are you still there?" Jonathan inquired after a few moments of silence.

"I'm here. Look, you scared me last night. You were aggressive, and you yelled at me, I'm not fond of that side of you at all. It frightened me. It can never happen again, Jonathan. I mean it!"

"Okay, so I have a bit of a temper, but doesn't everyone?"

"Look, we should sit down and talk. I need to explain some things to you, so you will better understand why your behavior bothered me so."

"Sure, Sarah. You make it sound so grave."

"It is, to me at least. I have to finish up some work for Mr. Thomas. Maybe we can meet for dinner tomorrow and talk some more."

"I was kind of hoping I would be able to see you tonight."

"No, Jonathan. Tonight I have a lot of thinking to do. I'll be in touch tomorrow. Have a good evening."

After she entered the last column of numbers in the general ledger and checked everything over, she placed the paperwork on the edge of Mr. Thomas's desk. He had left early in the afternoon to call on a new client.

"I'm going to go home now, Rita."

"Okay, sweetheart. I'll lock up."

"Are you working late, Rita?"

"Maybe for a bit. I need to catch up on some things. I like the peace and quiet of the office after everyone has left. It gives me time to breathe before I go home to my screaming brood."

"Okay then. Good night." Sarah often wondered why Rita didn't like going home, but she did understand wanting to have time to herself because that was the way she was feeling at the moment.

Rita's phone rang as Sarah opened the door to leave. Waving goodbye, Sarah shut the door and started walking toward the bus stop.

Rita answered the phone. Maybe it was one of her kids. "Hello, Thomas Finance Company. How may I help you?"

"Rita, it's Jonathan. We need to talk."

***

When Sarah arrived at the office the next morning, Rita was engrossed in a phone conversation, her hand cupped over the receiver. Sarah assumed it was a private conversation, so she settled in at her desk without wishing Rita a good morning.

"That's not what we agreed to," Sarah heard Rita say as her voice began to escalate. "I told you we were going to do it my way!" Slamming down the phone receiver, Rita sat with her head resting in her hands.

"Um…are you okay, Rita? I didn't mean to eavesdrop, but you seem very upset with the person to whom you were speaking."

"Oh that," Rita said, trying to brush it aside. "That was a young man who is getting too big for his britches."

"Is it your son, Daniel, again?"

"Daniel? Yes, of course," Rita said after a short pause. "Daniel is always getting himself into one kind of mess or another. It'll all work out. He is such an eager beaver to get a project done that he doesn't always consider the risks involved."

Sarah returned to her desk thinking what a good mother Rita was, always understanding Daniel's shortcomings.

The day went by without a peep from Rita. Before leaving the office that afternoon, Sarah tried approaching her once more. But Rita still appeared to be agitated from her conversation with her son. Not wanting to be the target of Rita's ire, she simply wished her a good night.

CHAPTER 18

The Big News

Sarah came in bright and early the next day, arriving before Rita. She gently knocked on her boss's office door, knowing that it was time to tell Mr. Thomas about her decision to take the position with Mr. Zimmerman.

"Come on in, Sarah. This must be serious. You have a somber look on your face."

"Um...yes, it is serious. Mr. Thomas, I've thought long and hard about this, and I want you to know how much I appreciate your taking a chance on me. I know you wanted two weeks' notice, and I'll give you that and more if you like..."

"Sarah, are you trying to tell me that you're going to accept the job with Zimmerman? Does he know yet?"

"Yes, Mr. Thomas, I am accepting the position. I feel as if I can really grow at his company. And no, I plan on calling Mr. Zimmerman later. I wanted you to be the first to know."

"I suppose it doesn't hurt that Zimmerman's handsome young nephew, Jonathan, is working there."

"Believe me, Mr. Thomas, at this point, Jonathan is as much a deterrent as he is a benefit."

"Trouble in paradise?"

"I don't know, Mr. Thomas. Sometimes he scares me."

Alarmed by what his young employee had just admitted to him, Roy Thomas knew he had to be careful how he phrased his next question. "Sarah, exactly how does he scare you? He didn't touch you, did he? Because if he has..." Mr. Thomas stopped midsentence, with his hands balled into fists at his side.

"Oh, no, Mr. Thomas. Jonathan hasn't physically hurt me. It has more to do with his behavior recently. He's become somewhat erratic. First, he's really sweet, then he's sarcastic, then he's hopping mad. I don't know which Jonathan I'm going to be spending time with anymore."

Not wanting to upset her further, Mr. Thomas decided to keep a closer watch over his soon-to-be former employee. "Sarah, I want you to keep in touch with me after you start your new job at Zimmerman Co. I mean it. I'd like to remain your mentor, so we'll need to speak at least once or twice a week."

"Oh, Mr. Thomas, I am honored that you want to be my mentor. Don't worry, you'll hear from me more often than you like."

"I doubt that, Sarah. Remember, call me about anything."

Thomas made a mental note to keep tabs on Jonathan. He wasn't going to tolerate any nonsense from that arrogant little nincompoop.

Sarah hadn't realized how long she and Mr. Thomas had been talking. She had gone into his office at 4:00 p.m., and it was almost 5:45 p.m. when she arrived back at her desk. She was running late. She had told Jonathan she would meet him at Benny's at 5:30 p.m. As she gathered her things and headed toward the door, she bumped into Jonathan. He looked like he was about to explode.

Do you know how worried I was about you?" he said putting his arms on the doorjamb, blocking her way.

"Why bother making a date if you're not going to show?"

"Jonathan, I had all intentions of showing up. I needed to speak with Mr. Thomas about something," she answered in an exasperated tone.

Roy Thomas heard a ruckus at the front door, and after seeing it was Jonathan, he knew he would have to confront him before he left the office with Sarah.

"What in all that is good do you think you're doing, Mr. Silver?"

Jonathan extended his hand, but Roy wasn't about to shake it.

"Sarah and I are having a discussion. I was worried about her because she was late for our date," said Jonathan through gritted teeth.

"Young man, Sarah was speaking with me, and that's why she was late," Mr. Thomas answered. "Now, I want you to remove your hand so that she can leave." He had to wait for a few tense moments before Jonathan did so. "You, Mr. Silver, are excused. You can leave my office now."

Staring at him in disbelief, Jonathan said, "Excused? Sarah and I have a date!"

"Why don't you ask the young lady about that?" Mr. Thomas saw the fear in Sarah's eyes.

"Look, Jonathan, I am sorry I was late, but your reaction is just over-the-top. I need some time to think. Let's reschedule our date for another night."

"No. We agreed to meet tonight. You said you had to explain something to me. Look, I know I sometimes get a little carried away, but I need to see you tonight. Please don't cancel. Please."

"Sarah, I can take you home if you like," offered Mr. Thomas, ignoring Jonathan's pleas.

"On second thought, maybe Jonathan and I should talk tonight. Thank you for the offer, Mr. Thomas, but I do have some things to say that Jonathan needs to hear, and the sooner the better."

"Okay, Sarah. I'd prefer to escort you home, but if you're sure about this—call me if you need me. Good night." He watched the two of them walk down the block. Every bone in his body told him to go after her, that Jonathan was not to be trusted.

CHAPTER 19

A Look into Henry

Benny's Kosher Deli was busy that night, but Sarah and
Jonathan managed to find a corner table away from much of
the noise.

"Sarah, again, I'm sorry about my earlier behavior," said
Johnathan. "I don't know what gets into me sometimes. You're just
so beautiful and…"

"Jonathan. Stop doing that. You always try to talk your way
out of bad behavior instead of taking responsibility for it. As long as
we're expressing our feelings, this seems like the perfect time for me
to explain why I find your behavior so disturbing."

"Disturbing? Look, Sarah, I was upset because you were late. I
already apologized."

"Jonathan, I need you to stop talking and just listen to me,
please."

"Okay already. I'm listening," said an irritated-looking Jonathan.

"You may have noticed that I haven't spoken much about my
father. There's a reason for that."

"Is he dead?"

"No, he's not dead. Henry is very much alive, although he may
as well be dead as far as my family is concerned. Now listen. Please!"

"Okay, but I'm not sure I understand, Sarah, you know, about your father."

"I'm getting there. Just stop interrupting me. Henry's mean. He has a hair-trigger temper, and his first impulse is to be harmful with his actions, his words, and his thoughts. He belittled and hit my mother, me, and my brothers on a daily basis. Bubbe would take me on vacation with her for ten weeks each summer to escape Henry. The first five weeks were spent at her cousin's farm in Ohio, and the last five with her siblings in the Catskills. Henry's a horrible man. Things got worse after my mother died when I was twelve."

Twelve. Rita never mentioned Sarah was so young when her mother died. He was fifteen when his own father died, and it left an indelible impression on him.

"Henry continued his physical rampages and even attacked my Bubbe. When I was fifteen, he abandoned us. He just left. We didn't have any money, we didn't know how we were going to take care of ourselves, or what was going to happen to the family. If it wasn't for my mother's family, I don't know what we would have done. My Bubbe told me it was a blessing in disguise. That even though he left us without a concern for our welfare, at least he was out of our lives. I prayed she was right. My grandmother and uncles came to our rescue. They helped pay our bills and made sure we had everything we needed."

"You have a great family, Sarah," Jonathan interjected.

"Yes, I do, Jonathan. They care a lot about me and my brothers. I'm not done with the story, though. There's more about Henry. When I was sixteen, he came back."

"Because he realized he did the wrong thing?"

"No, because he is such a jerk. He wanted to kick us out of one of the few places we could afford to live. It was a rental, but since his name was on the lease, he negotiated with the landlord. We had thirty days to vacate the premises. It was a horrible scene that day. Henry arrived unannounced. I was in the bedroom folding clothes, and I heard someone come in through the screen door. I knew Bubbe had gone out to the Jewish Home and thought she had returned. As I was walked down the hall, I could smell his cologne. It was Henry."

"What did you do?"

"He and I had words. Bubbe walked in a few moments later, and he ended up putting his hands on her. I ran to her defense, and Henry started to push me. He grabbed my arm and pushed me against the wall. When he was about to smack me…"

"Smack you?"

"Please just listen, Jonathan. This is difficult for me to talk about, and your constant interruptions are not making it any easier. Henry had just pushed me against the wall and was about to smack me in the face when my brother David, who was only twelve at the time, raced to my rescue. I was dazed from hitting the wall, and all I could do was look on in horror as Henry pummeled David. Afterward, David looked as if he had been hit by a ton of bricks. There wasn't an inch of him that didn't have a bruise on it. He just lay there. Henry stormed out of the door, angry that we had dared to defy him and screamed from the street that we better be out in thirty days. I wanted to call the hospital for an ambulance, but Bubbe didn't want me to draw any attention from the neighbors. After all, it was a family matter. I called my friend Mitzi. Her brother James drove us to the hospital. David was there for a week."

Seeing how distraught she was, Jonathan gently took Sarah's hand, rubbing his thumb along the top of her hand. He had done that in the past with his mother, and it always made her feel better, although Jonathan didn't quite understand why, as he was not comforted by the touch of another.

"What happened then?"

"Bubbe and my uncles decided to go to court to get custody of David. They suggested that my grandmother and I apply for joint custody. HaShem must have been watching over us because we won, Jonathan. We won custody of David from Henry. But that's when Henry took his revenge. I knew he was a horrible man. I just never thought that he would do such a thing!"

"What did he do?"

"He took Steven, my youngest brother, that's what! I was at school a few weeks after his unannounced visit when my grandmother contacted the school. I was asked to leave my Future

Bookkeepers meeting and go the principal's office. Bubbe was on the phone. She was crying so much I could hardly understand her. She told me Henry had taken Steven, my baby brother. He took him! I was so angry. Henry told my Bubbe that this was payback for taking custody of David away from him. And he kept him for two years until he grew tired of him. He came back into our lives just before I met you." Not sure where to focus her eyes, Sarah stared down at her hands.

Jonathan's mind was racing. What was he supposed to do with this information? This was so maudlin. What was Sarah telling him this for?

"Look, Sarah I can't imagine why anyone would want to hurt you, but what does this have to do with me, with us?"

Sarah was in shock. She realized Jonathan had not made the connection of what had happened to her with her father to how he was acting with her.

"When you scream at me, race off in your car like you did the other night, or bully me like you did earlier this evening, you scare me. When you do those things, you remind me of my father."

Jonathan jumped up from his seat. "Thanks a lot, Sarah. First, you're ornery about me letting the cat out of the bag about your big job announcement, and now you're comparing me to someone who abuses women and children. Nice. What's next? Are you going to start comparing me to murderers?"

His voice was escalating. Heads were turning, and Sarah was becoming uneasy. "Shhh…please sit down, Jonathan. You're embarrassing me."

"Embarrassing you…you just accused me of…"

"That's all you have to say! I pour my heart out to you, tell you that your behavior toward me concerns me because it reflects…"

The deli manager walked over to their table. "Is everything okay, miss?"

"Yes, it's fine. We're just having a discussion. Sorry, it got so loud."

"Okay, but if there's anything you need, just let me know." As he walked away, he nodded to Jonathan as if to tell him to behave himself. Jonathan seemed to pick up on the hint because he sat back down at the table.

"Take it easy. I didn't mean to diminish what you said. I get it. Your father's a real piece of work. You don't like him, and you're afraid I may have some of his less desirable characteristics. But you're wrong. Sure, I get upset every once in a while. Everyone does, even you, Sarah, but I'm not like your father. Look, I'll work on my temper. I promise, baby doll."

Sarah didn't believe a word he was saying, and it showed on her face. She had had enough of Jonathan for one night. Maybe she should have let Mr. Thomas bring her home after all. As she stood and grabbed her handbag from the chair, Jonathan took her hand.

"I want you to seriously consider my uncle's offer so we can work together. Then we won't have to worry about meeting each other and being late."

CHAPTER 20

Two Weeks' Notice

I was giving Mr. Thomas my resignation, and that's why I was late in meeting you," Sarah interjected. "I decided to accept your uncle's job offer."

"Ye-e-s-s-s! Does he know yet?"

"No, I planned on calling him in the morning. Why?"

"No reason. He's going to be so excited that you're on the Zimmerman team now."

"And how about you, Jonathan? Are you thrilled that I'm on the team now?"

"Of course, I am. You're my girl. I'll get to see you every minute of the day. Now, do you think you can you explain to me why old man Thomas looked like he was frothing at the mouth when he saw me talking to you in the doorway?"

"He was upset because you were screaming at me and blocking my way. Mr. Thomas is very protective of me, and I kind of like it," Sarah said playfully, sticking her tongue out at Jonathan.

"Hey, I care about you a whole lot more than old man Thomas does."

"Stop calling him that," Sarah said as she stomped her foot on the ground. "He's a very nice man. I'll miss him."

Sarah wanted the job with Mr. Zimmerman and hoped that Jonathan would be true to his word about controlling his temper because he could be the sweetest, kindest, gentlest man when he wanted to be. That's the Jonathan she loved, but he only showed up occasionally, these days. Maybe things would change when she started working at his uncle's firm—at least she hoped so.

***

There were times when Sarah needed to speak with Nate and only Nate, and this evening was one of them. Since she couldn't discuss Jonathan with Bubbe, she wanted to get Nate's opinion on the matter. Sarah decided to wait up for him to come home. She began reading but fell asleep.

"Hey, Sarah, shouldn't you be in bed?" asked Nate, as he repeatedly tapped on her shoulder.

"Oh, good you're home. I need to speak with you."

"What's going on?"

"Shhh, Nate. Bubbe is asleep in her room, and I don't want her to hear us talking. Oh, Nate. There's this guy, and I'm hung up on him. At least, I really liked him when I first met him, but now I'm not so sure, and Bubbe doesn't like him at all, and oh, I just don't know what to do."

"A guy? My little sister has a guy? So, what's this guy's name?"

"Jonathan."

"Jonathan got a last name?" Nate patted down his shirt to find his pen and paper. He would need this information so he could track down the guy if he ever hurt his sister.

"Umm…why do you need to know his last name? I know your temper, Nate. You're not going to hurt him, are you?"

"Hey, come on, Sarah. Since when am I the heavy? I'm just trying to find out about this new man in your life." *If he hurts her, I'll kill him*, he thought.

"You're not being helpful, Nate."

***

The next morning, Sarah called Mr. Zimmerman and told him the good news. He was ecstatic and welcomed her on board as the newest member of the Zimmerman team. Now all she had to do was tell Rita. She hoped she would understand and support her decision. Rita had become akin to a big sister to Sarah, ever since she began working at the Thomas Finance Co. two years ago. She would miss her terribly.

After getting off the phone, she realized that Rita hadn't arrived yet. *Where was she?* Rita was usually at the office by this time. She sat down at her desk and began transcribing a client letter when she heard the office door open. For an instant, she thought it was Jonathan. It smelled like his cologne, but when she turned around, it was Rita. Her imagination was playing games with her again.

"Good morning. I have some huge news for you, Rita."

"Don't tell me. Your father returned yet another family member." Leave it to Rita to inject sarcasm into the conversation.

"Rita! Stop that. No, it's not that at all. I told Mr. Thomas last night that I was accepting Mr. Zimmerman's offer to work at his company."

Rita had an odd expression on her face, almost as if she was aware of the news before hearing it. Sarah was puzzled.

"You look like you already know. Darn it. I wanted to be the first to tell you. Did Mr. Thomas call you to give you the news?"

"Oh no, dear, no one had to tell me. I knew from the moment you mentioned it to me that you were going to take the job. You just seem so enamored with Jonathan, and I think you mentioned that the job does pay more. I think it's wonderful. I'm so happy for you."

It sounded plausible, but something felt off. *It must be my nerves.*

***

Sarah had hoped that she and Rita could spend some time together before she started her new job, but every time she approached her, it seemed Rita was busy on the phone or about to run off to do something. Sarah began to feel as if her coworker wanted her to leave. *Had she done something to upset her?*

The last two weeks at Thomas Finance flew by. Sarah couldn't believe that today was her last day. It's not as if she would never see Mr. Thomas again. After all, he was Mr. Zimmerman's accountant, but it would be different for sure. She had never worked anywhere else, outside of the hours she put in at her uncle's gas station while she was still in high school. Now she was leaving for bigger and better opportunities—opportunities that didn't often open up for many young women, especially someone as young as Sarah.

Rita had been missing in action all day. Sarah hoped she would return before day's end so she could say so long to her friend.

Lost in her thoughts, she didn't hear Mr. Thomas call her name. "Sarah, yoo-hoo, Sarah. I've been calling you. I know as of Monday you no longer work for me, but you're still on my time for the next hour. Do you think you could meet me in the conference room?"

Startled, Sarah almost tripped on her own two feet as she got up from her desk. "Sorry, Mr. Thomas. I guess I was daydreaming."

Odd. The conference room door was closed. When he wasn't having a meeting, Mr. Thomas always left it open. As Sarah turned the knob, she heard snickers coming from the other side. What was so funny? Suddenly, she felt the door handle pull from the inside. It was Mr. Thomas. Swinging it open, she heard several people cheer "surprise."

Sarah couldn't believe her eyes. Mr. Thomas was surrounded by Rita, Mr. Zimmerman, and Jonathan.

"Happy going-away party," Rita yelled from across the room.

Sarah ran up to her and gave her a hug. "I'm going to miss you so much."

"Me too, kiddo. But we'll be in touch. Who am I going to moan to about my kids?"

"Did you get things resolved with Daniel?" Sarah asked.

"Daniel?" queried Rita.

"Yes, a few weeks ago, you had an argument with him on the phone, and when I asked about it, you said he was getting too big for his britches. Were you able to resolve the issue?"

"Oh that. Not a big deal. Just a little 'motherly' advice from me to him," she said, winking at Sarah.

After Sarah turned around, Rita saw Jonathan smirking. When he got closer to her, he whispered, "Your son, huh? That's what you told her?"

He was met by a cold stare from Rita.

CHAPTER 21

Shadows of Rose

S arah glanced at the large round clock on the wall above her
desk. It was 10:20 a.m., and Jonathan hadn't come to work yet.
He hadn't mentioned that he would be late this morning.

She had been working side by side with Jonathan since beginning at the Zimmerman Co. two months ago. At first, she wasn't
sure how things would work out, but Jonathan kept his promise. His
mood was more cheerful; he didn't explode like he had in the past.
He was back to the Jonathan she fell for so many months earlier…
her Mr. Dreamboat.

She breathed a little easier now that the friction between them
was a thing of the past. She wished she could say the same about
her relationship with Bubbe. She had never seen her grandmother as
upset as she was the night Sarah told her that she had accepted Mr.
Zimmerman's job offer. They had just finished their evening meal.
David and Steven excused themselves, cleared their plates, and went
into the living room to listen to the radio before going to bed. That
left Sarah and Bubbe to clean up. Sarah started to wash the dishes,
and her grandmother grabbed a dish towel to dry them. She was
trying to figure out how to bring up the topic, but her grandmother
beat her to it.

"Sarah, you've been so quiet lately. Is anything vrong?"

"No, Bubbe, everything is fine. Actually, I have some exciting news."

"News? Tell me. Did Mr. Thomas give you a raise?"

"Well, you're partially right. I did get a raise, but not from Mr. Thomas."

"I don't understand."

"Mr. Zimmerman offered me a job at his company, and I'll be working more closely with Jonathan. I've known about it for a while, but I wasn't sure if I was going to accept it or not and…"

"No!" Bubbe threw down the dishrag. "No, no, no, no, no!" she continued as she stomped out of the kitchen and into the living room. Both David and Steven turned toward their grandmother to see what the commotion was about. Bubbe stood there, red in the face, hands on her hips.

"David. Steven. Go schlafen now. Your sister and I have some things to discuss."

As Steven got up and walked toward his bedroom, David remained on the couch, with his hands behind his head. "I'm not tired right now. It's too early for bed. Besides, I don't want to miss anything, Bubbe."

"David Heschel Steinman!" David had never seen Bubbe so upset and, for a moment, just stared back at her bewildered.

"Now!" his grandmother bellowed.

Hearing Bubbe's outburst, Sarah ran into the living room, just as David stomped off to his room, slamming the door shut behind him.

Sarah broke the silence. "Bubbe, I wish you wouldn't get yourself so worked up. This is a wonderful opportunity for me. Mr. Zimmerman has given me responsibilities I never dreamed of having, and Jonathan has been such a mensch."

Before she could get another syllable out of her mouth, Bubbe threw her hands up in the air, signaling Sarah to stop talking. Her grandmother just stared at her with tears filling her eyes.

Wiping her palms on her apron, Molly drew in a long, deep breath, exhaled, and sat down on the couch.

"Sarah, sit. Ve need to talk. You have grown into such a lovely young voman. Ve are all so proud of you and your accomplishments. I don't ever vant you to think you have to settle for someone who doesn't treat you like a queen."

"I won't," Sarah responded quietly. Did Bubbe think she lacked all judgment? She wasn't a child after all.

"Good. Good. I am happy you have a better job, but you hid it from me. Up until you met Jonathan, you told me everything. But now I feel you pulling away. I don't like that feeling. My Rose did the same thing vhen she met Henry."

Sarah sat there not knowing what to say. Why did Bubbe have to keep bringing this up? She wasn't her mother. Jonathan wasn't Henry. Okay, so he had a bad temper, but he never hit her. He never became as vile as Henry.

"I know you don't think you're like your mama and that Jonathan is nothing like Henry."

Sarah wondered if Bubbe could read her mind; that's exactly what she was thinking.

"I just don't vant to see you make the same mistakes my Rose did. It killed me seeing vhat he did to her."

Pointing to her chest, she said, "She died inside here before the good Lord took her. I von't allow you to have such an awful fate."

Sarah's mind was reeling. She didn't know what to think. All she knew was that she had to end this conversation before it went any further.

"Bubbe, I know you're upset with me, but can we have this conversation another time, another day? I promise one day soon, I'll sit, and you can tell me about Rose and Henry, but right now I'm tired, and I need to get some sleep. Besides, this isn't a matter of life or death."

"I know it isn't something you vant to hear, but you have to hear it. Ve are going to have a talk about this soon." Molly knew her granddaughter didn't realize just how wrong she was about Jonathan. As far as Bubbe was concerned, she was in a battle with Jonathan for Sarah's soul. And she had every intention of being the victor.

From that evening on, Sarah avoided speaking with her grandmother about anything that even hinted it was going in that direction. She realized that she and Bubbe were never going to see eye to eye about Jonathan.

CHAPTER 22

It's a Surprise

S arah? Sarah?" Jonathan said, snapping his fingers in front of her face. "Hey, gorgeous, what's going on?"

"Oh. Sorry. I was just thinking about the tension between Bubbe and me."

"Is that all? Listen, she's just being overprotective. And she is getting on in years, maybe all this is the first sign of senility."

"Don't say that, Jonathan. Don't even joke about that. By the way, what took you so long to get here today? I thought you were going to come in earlier?"

"Keeping tabs on me already? Geez, Sarah, we're not even engaged yet. Give a guy a break."

"If it's a break you need, Jonathan…"

"Don't get all upset. I was late because I was planning a special surprise for you, for later."

"Surprise? What surprise?"

"Oh no, I get to have my little secrets."

Hell, he winced. Why did he have to say a surprise. Now he was going to have to come up with something for this evening. Maybe Rita would have an idea.

"What are you working on, doll?"

"Your uncle asked me to review the accounts payable and receivable for the last few years…you know, just to make sure everything is in order."

"Why wouldn't it be in order?" asked Jonathan. "I'm in charge of entering the accounts, and I don't make mistakes. And those errors you found earlier this year were a fluke. There's no way anyone was taking that amount of money under my watch. We didn't have any of these problems when Rita was checking our books. Then you get the job, and suddenly there's trouble. I don't know what you and my uncle are cooking up, Sarah, but I'm not going to let it go on."

Listening to Jonathan's tirade, she wondered when and why meshuganah Jonathan had reentered the picture, and what had happened to her Mr. Dreamy? She was not going to let him intimidate her—not this time.

"Jonathan, Mr. Zimmerman, your uncle and my boss, and by the way the owner of this firm, asked me to look over some numbers. I'm not trying to pull anything. I don't know why you're getting so upset. If you have a problem with your uncle—talk to him!"

"That's exactly what I plan on doing," he muttered as he walked toward his uncle's office. Once Jonathan went into the office, Sarah couldn't hear what was going on, and to be truthful, she didn't care much. Jonathan may be the heir apparent, but he wasn't her supervisor. She was still taking orders from Mr. Zimmerman.

Sarah was busy working on the books when she heard her boss's office door slam. Jonathan looked extremely unhappy. He didn't even acknowledge her before he walked out the front door.

Then, her desk phone rang. "Hello. Yes, Mr. Zimmerman. I'll be right there." What did Jonathan do now? she wondered.

***

Mr. Zimmerman was on the phone when Sarah entered his office. He pointed for her to sit down in a chair on the opposite side of the desk.

"Yes, thank you. I appreciate that," he said as he hung up the phone. "Sarah, don't look so scared. I'm not upset with you. In fact,

I want to tell you how pleased I am with the quality of your work. I wish my nephew had half the work ethic you do. Have you had a chance to complete the review of the ledgers I asked for?"

"I'll need a bit more time, Mr. Zimmerman. There's a lot to get through."

"Did anything pop up that I should know about?" Mr. Zimmerman asked.

"Before I say anything, I'd like to review the numbers again…if that's okay with you, Mr. Zimmerman."

"Absolutely, but I'd like a report in the next few days."

"I know it's not any of my business, but can I ask why Jonathan stormed out of the office a little while ago? His whole mood changed when I told him you had asked me to review the books again. Did I do something wrong? Was that his job? Because I don't want to take anything away from Jonathan. I don't like it when he's upset like this."

"Let's talk in the morning, Sarah. If you see my nephew, tell him I'm docking a day's pay from his check this week."

"If you don't mind, sir, I think I'll give you the pleasure of relaying that information to him."

CHAPTER 23

Daniel's Account

Sarah had completed her review of the books and was ready to deliver the accounts to Mr. Zimmerman. There were several inconsistencies, including seven entries made by Jonathan. Sarah knew this because his initials J.S. were on the right side of the column. Everyone who entered a check amount had to initial it. There were checks to several vendors with whom Sarah was not familiar, but the sore thumb in the group was the twelve thousand dollars' worth of checks made out to Daniel Polansky. Rita had a son named Daniel Polansky. It had to be a coincidence. Why would Jonathan—even meshuganah Jonathan—write out multiple checks to Rita's son? And were the other six companies that Jonathan had signed off on legit? The more she looked at the books, the more questions she had.

After the argument with his uncle, Jonathan needed some encouragement. "Hi, Rita, it's your lover boy."

"I know that tone. What did you mess up now, Jonathan? Did something happen between the time we spoke yesterday and now?"

"Sarah happened."

"Explain," said Rita.

"Okay, so I went into work. Before I got a chance to say anything, Sarah was on me about being late. I had to think of something and quick. I told her I was planning a surprise for her for later.

You've got to help me. I have no idea what to do. Oh, and then she tells me that my uncle has asked her to review the accounts again."

"So?"

"I may have written out a few checks in your son Daniel's name over the last year."

"My Daniel? Why would you do something asinine like that?" asked Rita, trying to keep her voice down.

"I needed to mix things up. I thought of Daniel starting college in a year or so, and figured I could always say it was to set up a college account for him. I'm going to own the company one day anyway. So technically, it's my money."

"You are such a spoiled brat and not a very bright one at that. Let me explain this to you once more. We have a plan, Jonathan. You make checks out to the bogus companies I have set up, not to anyone who can be traced to you or me. I suggest you fix this now."

"But Sarah has already seen it. What do you expect…"

"You'll think of something, Jonathan. Because if I go down, sweetheart, you are coming with me," she said, slamming down the phone receiver.

Her office phone rang again. Rita knew it was Jonathan. "What?"

"I need your help in figuring out what kind of surprise I should plan for Sarah tonight."

"You really are a lost cause."

"You're not helping, Rita."

"That's because right now I'm not in the mood to help you!"

Rita was incensed. *Darn him! What the heck was he thinking? Jonathan is getting a little too big for his britches. Is he trying to ruin everything? How careless can he be, putting money in my son Daniel's name? I'm going to have to show him who has the real power in our relationship. This situation is getting out of hand. He can't be that stupid. Or maybe it isn't stupidity at all. Maybe he is falling for Sarah. The* thought made Rita giggle. Oh…oh…oh that's rich. Jonathan and pure little Sarah. Jonathan doesn't have a sincere bone in his body.

***

That evening, Sarah was busy getting ready for her date with Jonathan, a date she wasn't even sure she wanted to keep, after his tirade at work earlier in the day.

"You're going out tonight, sweetheart?" asked her grandmother. "Bubbe, I told you I have a date with Jonathan. Now, before you say anything, I know he's been a little odd lately, but he's been under a lot of stress. He doesn't mean to take it out on me. He would never hurt me. Bubbe, you have to believe that."

"Sarah, I learned a long time ago that people show their true colors vhen they are angry. He should never take his anger out on you. You know I have concerns about Jonathan, but you're a young voman now, and I can't make decisions for you. I can only ask that you vatch out and not jump into anything. By the way, vhere is Jonathan taking you this evening? I hope it's Kashrut.

"He promised it was kosher, but he won't tell me the name of the restaurant. I'm so excited. Jonathan told me he has a surprise for me."

Molly could feel her blood pressure rising.

"Bubbe, what's wrong? You don't look so well. Are you okay?"

Molly didn't know how to respond to her granddaughter. Should she tell her about the thoughts that were reeling through her head? No, it was best not to say anything.

"I'm fine, Sarah. Have a vonderful time tonight and remember vhat I said."

Hearing a knock at the door, Molly called to her granddaughter: "I think it's him. I vill get the door vhile you finish getting ready, Sarah."

Bubbe opened the door and there stood Jonathan dressed to the nines, looking perfect. A little too perfect.

"Hello, Mrs. Roth. Is your beautiful granddaughter ready for a night on the town?"

Molly wanted to scream, "No. Never. She's never going to be ready to go out with you. Leave now," but instead she answered, "She's nearly ready, Mr. Silver. Come sit down."

"Sure thing." Jonathan was ill at ease with Sarah's grandmother. It was as if she knew what he was thinking. *Nah, it's only your imagination. She's an old hag.*

"Jonathan, Sarah tells me you have a surprise for her tonight."

"Yes, I sure do."

"Is it a surprise I'm going to be happy about, Mr. Silver?" Molly secretly hoped Jonathan was planning to break up with Sarah, but she knew that it was unlikely to happen.

"I guess you'll have to wait and see."

"Yes, yes, Mr. Silver, ve vill see."

As Sarah entered the room Jonathan gazed at her with admiration, extended his hand and said: "Sarah, you look great. All set to go to dinner?"

Sarah wasn't at all sure how this date was going to end up, but she was willing to give it a go. "All set, Jonathan. Bye, Bubbe. Love you," Sarah said as she walked out the door arm in arm with Jonathan.

Once they left the apartment, Molly panicked. She called Robert. Out of all her boys, he was the one who could always calm her down.

"Hi, Mom. Is something wrong?"

"Vhy vould you think anything is vrong? Can't I call my son and say allo?"

"Okay, Mom, what's wrong? I know something is going on because I can hear it in your voice. What is it? Is David causing a problem again? Is something going on with Steven?"

"No, Robert; the boys are good. They're good. I'm calling about Sarah."

"What's wrong with Sarah? What happened, Mom?"

"It's not vhat happened. It's vhat is going to happen. I can feel it in my bones."

"Mom, I thought we talked about this. Stop getting yourself worked up about what hasn't even happened. It just raises your blood pressure, and you know what the doctor said…"

"Enough. I'm eighty-seven years old, and I know vhen I should trust my feelings and vhen I shouldn't. Don't tell me not to get upset. That little...schmendrik is going to take my granddaughter avay from me. Just like my Rose vas taken away from me. I can't let it happen again, Robert. Not again."

"Mom, I'm coming over. Let's sit and talk about this rationally."

"I'll make a bisl tea."

CHAPTER 24

Out on the Town

Jonathan pulled his car up to the restaurant valet, Sarah looked on with wonderment. It was Le Francais, the new French kosher restaurant Sarah had heard about. Could Jonathan afford this? Walking through the double mahogany doors, she stepped into an elegance that she had never experienced before. As the waiter pulled out her chair, Sarah marveled at the furnishings and romantic ambiance: the brocade drapes, the color of burgundy, and the beautiful murals of the French countryside on the walls. The cherrywood chairs with seats that matched the burgundy brocade on the draperies were every bit of luxury.

"Sarah? Sarah?" Jonathan asked, waving his hand in front of Sarah's face.

"Sorry. I was just appreciating the beauty in this restaurant. Thank you for bringing me here, Jonathan. I've never been to such an elegant place before. Is this the surprise?"

"Uh-uh, you have to wait for the surprise. Besides, nothing in this place can ever compare with your beauty."

"Jonathan, that is so sweet." Sarah could feel her face heat up as it changed to various shades of crimson. "Honestly, after this morning, I was thinking about canceling our date, but I'm glad I didn't.

"You what?"

"Good evening. I'm Raphael, and I'll be your waiter this evening. What may I get you to drink?"

"Your best champagne," said Jonathan, still steaming about Sarah's last comment. He decided it was best to stick to his plan.

"Have you lost your mind?" Sarah asked in a whispered tone. "That sounds awfully expensive. Besides, I'm not even legal yet."

"Stop getting upset about everything, Sarah. Try to enjoy yourself."

When the waiter returned with their champagne, they ordered dinner. Sarah ordered the trout almondine dry, without any sauce. She had to watch her weight after all, and Jonathan ordered the rib eye steak with all the trimmings. While waiting for their meal to arrive, Jonathan held Sarah's hand, sharing jokes and stories about his college days.

Although Sarah loved hearing these stories, she was also a little jealous of Jonathan's being able to attend college. Under her current circumstances, that was next to impossible. She was wondering what it would be like to have the opportunity to go to college, when she realized she missed a part of Jonathan's story as he said the punch line.

"After that he never looked at a cow the same way," said Jonathan, looking like he was about to burst at the seams with laughter. "Poor guy, he still can't eat beef."

Just as the story ended, Raphael appeared with their food. "Perfect timing," said Jonathan. "I just told this lovely lady my funniest story, and I didn't know how I was going to top that. You came to my rescue."

Did Jonathan just wink at the waiter as he said "top that"? Sarah wondered.

Sarah's face was aching; she had been smiling all night. This was the Jonathan she had fallen in love with. The man who made her laugh and made her feel special. Well, except for his untimely tirades here and there.

"Dinner was delicious, Jonathan. Thank you, again."

"Well, we're not done yet, Sarah. We still have dessert and the surprise. Besides, you haven't finished your champagne."

"I don't think I can eat or drink another drop. I took a sip of the champagne earlier, but it tickled my nose."

Sarah may not have been drinking, but Jonathan was starting to feel inebriated after his fourth glass of champagne. He needed the inflated sense of courage that the alcohol gave him to go through with Sarah's surprise. Truth be told, he wasn't hungry for dessert either, but it was all part of the plan.

"Let's get something we can share," Jonathan suggested. "They have great sorbet here."

"Whatever you want, Jonathan."

"Mademoiselle and monsieur, would you like to order dessert?"

"Yes, we'd like to share the sorbet," said Jonathan. "Sarah, please excuse me. I'll be right back. Nature calls."

Jonathan took the opportunity to peek his head in the kitchen and ask the chef if he would be able to put the diamond ring he held in his hand on top of the sorbet.

He returned to the table as Raphael was serving the dessert. The sorbet was showcased on a glass plate with a silver lid covering it. As the lid was lifted, Sarah gasped. A flawless, one-carat, round solitaire ring, set in platinum, sat on top of their dessert. Sarah's eyes went from the diamond to Jonathan. She couldn't breathe.

Scooping the ring up with his spoon and wiping it off on the napkin, Jonathan got down on one knee.

"Sarah Steinman, will you marry me?"

This was not the surprise Sarah had expected. Not even close. "Jonathan, you sure know how to surprise a girl. You know I care about you, right? It's just that we've only known each other a few months, and we've had our ups and downs. You just blew up at me this morning. How could you even consider marriage?" Her head was spinning. *Why was he trying to rush things?* "Can't we wait a bit until things progress a little more? You know how complicated my life is. I can't even think about marriage right now."

And then there was silence. Jonathan stood up, looming over Sarah who was still sitting in her chair. She watched his face change in what seemed like seconds. His lips tightened, almost disappearing on his face. His brow furrowed. She was overcome with fear. Not taking his eyes off her, he grabbed the ring and put it into the inner pocket of his jacket. Without saying a word, he turned on his heels and headed toward the door. Sarah was dumbfounded.

"Would the lady like another glass of champagne?" asked the waiter.

"Champagne? No, thank you. Did the gentleman I was with happen to pay for dinner?"

"No, mademoiselle, he did not. Is there a problem?"

There was a problem all right. That jerk had left her with the bill. Jonathan hadn't changed at all. "No, not at all. Would it be possible for me to use the maître d's phone?"

"Certainly. I shall bring it over to your table."

Raphael returned with the phone in hand, followed by a very long cord. Sarah's first thought was to call Mitzi, but she was too embarrassed. Mitzi had warned her about Jonathan's less than palatable behaviors of late. Instead, she dialed Mr. Thomas's number. He did say to call if she needed him. And right now, she definitely needed him.

"Mr. Thomas. Hi, it's Sarah. I know it's late, but I need your help. Jonathan and I were out to dinner and he…"

"Just tell me where you are, Sarah," interrupted Mr. Thomas. "You can explain the rest when I get there."

Sitting at the table, Sarah was going over everything that happened with Jonathan the last several months when she felt a hand touch her shoulder.

"Sarah, are you okay?" asked Mr. Thomas.

"Oh, Mr. Thomas." That was all she was able to get out before the tears started flowing.

"Okay, Sarah, what's wrong? What did that imbecile do to you, and where the heck is he now!"

"Jonathan proposed to me, and ahh, I said no. It was just too soon. He looked so angry and left. He didn't even bother to pay the bill, and I didn't bring enough money with me and, and…" Sarah began crying all over again.

"You stay here while I take care of this." She watched as Mr. Thomas walked over to the waiter and paid the bill. What would she have done without Mr. Thomas?

"Come on, Sarah." Mr. Thomas helped her on with her coat, put his arm around her shoulder, and led her to his car. The car ride seemed like it lasted forever, even though it was only fifteen minutes long. Arriving at her building, Mr. Thomas insisted on walking Sarah upstairs. As they reached the apartment door, Sarah turned toward him. "Mr. Thomas, I'll pay you back for the dinner, I promise. I just didn't know what to do…"

Mr. Thomas gently placed his hands on Sarah's shoulders. "You needed help, and I'm glad you called me. Don't worry about paying me back. I'll get payment from Jonathan. And I'm going to enjoy making that little idiot sweat. Have a good night, Sarah, and don't worry about it."

When Sarah walked into the apartment, it was dark, except for the light from a small lamp in the living room. Bubbe always left the light on in case anyone had to get up in the middle of the night.

CHAPTER 25

The Morning After

S arah woke up to the sound of the phone ringing. She grabbed her watch. It was 6:00 a.m. Although this was typically the time she woke up to get ready for work, it was too early for anyone to call. She jumped out of bed, hoping to get to the phone before it disturbed Bubbe or the boys. But before she could reach it, Steven had answered the phone.

"Hello, Steinman residence."

"Is Sarah there?"

"Who's calling?"

"Can you just get Sarah? I don't have time for small talk."

"I'll take that, Steven," Sarah said as she snatched the phone receiver out of his hand.

"Hello, this is Sarah."

"Sarah, it's Jonathan."

Of course, it is. He was the only person she knew rude enough to call someone at six o'clock in the morning.

"Did you have a difficult time getting home last night? I bet you called old man Thomas for help."

"And I bet you think it's funny that you left a girl with a very large bill, at that fancy restaurant, and no way to get home!"

"Serves you right," said Jonathan. "Who do you think you are turning me down? Do you know how important my family is? How marrying me could have brought you up in the world?"

Sarah was at a loss for words.

"Are you there?!" he screamed. "Oh, and don't bother showing up at work today. After I tell my uncle what happened, you won't have a job!"

She was going to show up at work regardless of Jonathan's rantings. Mr. Zimmerman was her boss, not Jonathan, and especially not this meshuga, unstable version of Jonathan. Besides, she wanted to ask Jonathan why he had made out several checks, totaling twelve thousand dollars, to Daniel Polansky.

After getting off the phone and being inundated with questions from Steven, none of which she answered, Sarah showered and got ready for work. She had hoped to leave without waking Bubbe. That way, she wouldn't have to lie to her about last night.

She did her best to be quiet, but somehow Bubbe always knew when she was about to leave. She felt her grandmother's hand rest gently on her arm. "Sarah, how vas your date last night? Vhat vas the big surprise?"

"The surprise? Oh, Jonathan took me to a beautiful restaurant, Bubbe. It was gorgeous. Listen, I'm rushed this morning, but I'll fill you in on all the details tonight," said Sarah as the door closed behind her.

***

Sarah arrived at the bus stop just as Charlie was about to pull away from the curb. He stopped to let her on.

"Good mornin', Sarah."

"Morning, Charlie."

"You, okay?"

"Sure am, Charlie." That was a lie. Sarah didn't feel okay. She found a seat near the middle of the bus and was so focused on what she was going to say and do when she got to work that she almost missed her stop.

"Sarah! You get off at Main Street, don't ya?"

"Oh, oh, yes. Thanks, Charlie," she said scrambling to her feet. She quickly exited the bus.

***

As she entered the office, Sarah saw Jonathan speaking with his uncle behind closed doors. Jonathan was sitting in a chair opposite his uncle's desk. Mr. Zimmerman was standing up, facing the glass door of his office. When he saw her, he waved for her to come in.

This must be what walking the gang plank feels like, she thought. Before she even entered the office, she could hear Mr. Zimmerman speaking in a clipped tone to Jonathan.

"No one…no one…tells me who to hire or fire. This may be your company one day, and at this moment that's even debatable, but what's not is that, right now, it's still in my name!"

Sarah stood with the door open and her heart in her throat. Jonathan was red-faced.

"Sarah, come in and sit down," said Mr. Zimmerman.

Sarah sat on the couch catty-corner from her boss's desk, far enough away from Jonathan so she could think straight.

"Look, I don't know what happened between the two of you, but work it out. I have a business to run, and I need you both focused so I can do just that. So, whatever it is, work it out! Now, both of you, out of my office."

Sarah got up to leave the office first, but Jonathan, who appeared to be on a mission, barged right passed her. No surprise. He was being a jerk again.

Jonathan's attitude remained icy for several days after that meeting. Sarah tried starting conversations with him, but he ignored her. She cared deeply for him, but if this was the way he wanted to handle things, she wasn't going to wallow in it. *Maybe Bubbe was right after all. Maybe Jonathan wasn't the one.*

However, not having him hovering over her was a perk. It gave her more time to focus on those accounting discrepancies she had come across. The problem was she needed to ask him some questions about it, and he wasn't likely going to want to answer them. She'd have to find the answers another way. *Rita! Rita would know.* Sarah dialed her direct number at Thomas Finance Co.

CHAPTER 26

Recruiting Help

There's more than one way to solve a puzzle. Rita had worked on the Zimmerman accounts before Sarah. She might have some insight and some answers as to why checks for such large amounts of money were being made out and initialed by Jonathan.

"Hello, Rita. It's Sarah. I'm fine. Do you have time to meet? I need to speak with you about something important. Great. See you then."

Rita had just gotten off the phone. With whom Roy Thomas wasn't sure, but she appeared deep in thought. Watching her stand at her desk, holding the phone receiver under her chin, she looked a lot like Rodin's The Thinker. *Rita is a character all right, but she is a good employee*, thought Roy, as he directed his attention back toward his adding machine.

Rita was rattled after Sarah's phone call. *Tea, that's what I need—a good cup of tea to settle my nerves. Why* was she nervous? All Sarah wanted to do was meet. Then why did the very thought of it makes the little hairs on her neck stand at attention? If Jonathan did anything to screw up their plan, she was going to have his head. He had already veered away from it when he made large payments to an account with her son's name. She didn't even want to think about what he may have confided in dear, sweet Sarah.

Rita could hear the phone on her desk ringing. *Maybe it is Sarah again*, she thought. Instead, she was met with a barrage of angry comments from Jonathan.

"Are you quite done, Jonathan? I've had about enough of your hissy fits lately," she added, cupping her hand around the receiver so Mr. Thomas wouldn't hear her conversation. "Because if you don't, you're going to ruin everything!"

"No, I'm not the one who is going to ruin everything. Sarah is!"

"Not if you keep her under control, just like we discussed, Jonathan."

"I tried to do that! Would you like to know what I did?" He knew full well that telling Rita about the proposal would drive her crazy. *She deserved it. She was being ungrateful. It was his family's money after all.*

Rita was curious. What was Jonathan trying to pull this time? "Okay, I give. What did you do, dear Jonathan?"

"I proposed."

"Proposed what? To whom?"

"Marriage! I proposed marriage to Sarah. There, I said it. Okay!"

"You proposed?" Rita could her blood pressure rising and a whopper of a headache coming on.

"I asked you to help me figure out a surprise for Sarah, and you hung up on me!"

"Son of a bee!" said Rita as she slammed down the receiver, ending her phone call with Jonathan.

Mr. Thomas almost fell out of his chair when he heard Rita yell into her phone. In all the time she had worked for him, Rita had always been in control of her emotions. He could not remember ever hearing her raise her voice—not once.

Rita was in such a panic that she didn't even notice Mr. Thomas walk up to her desk.

"Are you okay, Rita? That's the first time I've heard you get upset. I sure wouldn't want to be the guy or gal on the other end of that conversation."

"Sorry about that, Mr. Thomas. Someone I trusted showed me that he is not worthy of that trust. Live and learn, right?"

CHAPTER 27

Rita's Help

Sarah didn't mention to Mr. Zimmerman that she was going ask Rita to help her unravel the Daniel Polansky mystery. She wanted to meet with her first. They had planned to have lunch near the boathouse in the park. Rita was fifteen minutes late.

Does that mean she has changed her mind and decided not to help? She was so deep in thought that she didn't initially notice when Rita arrived. She was out of breath, but she was there.

"Sorry, I'm late, Sarah. At the last minute, Mr. Thomas asked me to stop at the post office."

"In that case, you're excused. Mr. Thomas has been my savior this week."

"Your savior?"

"Yes. The short version of a very long story is that Jonathan took me out to a lovely dinner and then proposed."

"Proposed? How lovely. I suppose congratulations are in order then. To you and Jonathan," Rita said, lifting her bottle of Coke. "But I don't see a ring on your finger?"

"That's where Mr. Thomas comes in. You see, Jonathan proposed, but I couldn't say yes. It's just too soon, Rita. I mean, I'm crazy about him, but between his moodiness and his disappearing acts, I don't feel we're ready yet. When I said no, Jonathan looked so angry and stormed out of the restaurant. I had to call Mr. Thomas to come and get me and pay the bill. I was so embarrassed, but what was I going to do?"

Rita stared at Sarah with her mouth agape and then began to laugh. "Wait a minute. Just hold your horses, and wait a minute! You're telling me Jonathan took you out to a fancy restaurant and proposed marriage to you, and you turned him down! I would have loved to have been a fly on that wall."

"Rita, it's not funny. I feel terrible about having to say no to Jonathan. He was so angry he tried to get me fired."

"Did Mr. Zimmerman fire you?" asked Rita.

"No, of course not. I don't think Jonathan told him that he proposed or that I said no, only that he couldn't work with me any longer. Mr. Zimmerman told us to work it out. Jonathan hasn't spoken to me since, and that's the reason I called you. You see, I need answers to some questions about certain accounts, and I thought since you had worked on them in the past, you'd be able to help me. Well, what do you say? Will you help me?"

"Sarah," said Rita patting her hand, "you know I would do anything for you."

"I'm so happy to hear you say that, Rita. Here's what I need to know. Jonathan has written checks to a vendor who has the same name as your son, Daniel."

"You know Daniel has helped Jonathan on and off, delivering packages and doing other small tasks. Maybe that was what the checks were for?"

"I don't think so, Rita. The checks are for thousands of dollars, twelve thousand dollars in all."

"Have you asked Jonathan about it?"

"I'd love to do just that, Rita, but he won't speak to me. I do need your help on this."

"Okay, why don't you bring the books over to the office tomorrow night, and we can go through them?"

"Great, thanks so much, Rita."

***

"Let's see what we have here."

Rita sat with Sarah, for forty-five minutes, meticulously going through the accounts. They compared the amounts in the signature ledger where vendor checks, were recorded and signed for, to those in the general ledger. Sarah watched as Rita adjusted her glasses, which slipped down her nose several times.

Finally, she looked up at Sarah and said, "You're right, something fishy is going on."

"That's what I thought. Some of these dates go back to when you were checking these accounts. Didn't you notice any of these discrepancies at the time?"

"Look, Sarah. I know you want to find out who is stealing money from Mr. Zimmerman, but don't try to turn the tables on me."

The last thing Sarah wanted to do was offend Rita. "Oh no, Rita. I wasn't implying anything at all. I just was curious, that's all. I do appreciate all the help you're giving me with this. And I know your bookkeeping skills are top-notch."

"Young people. You think you know everything. Let's forget this conversation ever happened. Why don't I get us some tea and cookies?" said Rita.

CHAPTER 28

It's MY Company

Jonathan was feeling so stilted by the refusal of his proposal that he didn't return to the office for work the next day. The morning he did, he noticed Sarah wasn't at her desk. He may not have been able to see her, but he could hear her, muffled as it was. She was in his Uncle Leonard's office chatting away. He knew she was talking about him, and he needed to know what was being said. He knocked on the office door, and when there was no answer, he opened it.

"You aren't talking about me behind my back now, are you?"

"Jonathan, Sarah and I are meeting about some problem areas on the general ledger, and I'd appreciate it if you wouldn't interrupt."

"This is going to be my company one day. I think I should be in on this meeting."

Sarah could feel her body stiffening. Her eyes wandered between Jonathan and his uncle, waiting to see who would speak first.

"Mr. Zimmerman, I can meet with you later," she said, jumping up from the armchair. "You and Jon…"

Mr. Zimmerman stared intently at his nephew, responding in a soft but measured tone. "Whether or not this becomes your company is yet to be seen, young man. Now, I want to speak with Sarah, alone. You and I can talk in a bit. Close the door behind you, Jonathan."

Furious at being dismissed like a schoolboy, Jonathan stomped out of the room.

Without missing a beat, Mr. Zimmerman turned his attention back to Sarah. "So, you were saying that there's a problem with things adding up in the general ledger and that this has been going on for about two years?"

"Yes, sir. I've gone over this numerous times. I even…"

"You even what, Sarah?"

"I hope you don't mind, Mr. Zimmerman, but if there is anyone who knows these books better than I do, it's Rita. She's been helping me review them. I figured two pairs of eyes are better than one."

"That's fine. I don't mind if Rita helps you. Roy Thomas is my accountant, and anyone in his office is golden. Although I wonder…"

Sarah sat on the edge of her seat, waiting for Mr. Zimmerman to complete his sentence.

"I wonder why Rita never caught onto this," he wondered aloud. "In all the time she balanced out my books, she never made any indication that there might be something awry. Don't you find that odd?"

Odd? Heck yeah, it was odd. She had asked Rita the same questions, and Rita had, in turn, made her feel like she was being ungrateful for asking. Then again, if she told Mr. Zimmerman that, it might get Rita into trouble. "Rita's good at what she does, Mr. Zimmerman, and we all make mistakes. Sometimes a fresh pair of eyes can see errors that haven't been noticed by those who have looked at something hundreds of times."

"You're a loyal friend, Sarah. Let's talk some more about this in a few days."

When Sarah left his office, Zimmerman sat down and dialed Roy Thomas.

"You old son of a gun. How are you, Leonard?" Roy asked. "I haven't seen much of you since you stole my bookkeeper. How is Sarah?"

"She's doing great, Roy. Just like I knew she would. I've been having her dig a little deeper into the accounting problem we were driving ourselves crazy about a few months ago."

Roy listened as Leonard Zimmerman went on explaining the discrepancies. He could feel a headache coming on, and this one was going to be a whopper. The pressure was building behind his eyes. Using his thumb and index finger, he pressed on the bridge of his nose to ease the throbbing pain while Leonard laid out the situation.

"Well, Roy, what do you think?"

"Quite a conundrum. It's got to be someone in your company. Don't you think?"

"That's what I've been scratching my head about. I don't know who it could be, but that's only part of the reason I called. You know I've always trusted you with our accounting, Roy, but I need to ask you something about Rita.

"What about her?" Roy asked.

"Well, and I'm not accusing her of anything, but Sarah has been digging back a couple of years, and there seems to be discrepancies throughout. Why do you think Rita never picked up on that Roy?"

You could hear a pin drop, and that made Leonard even more anxious. "Roy? Are you there, buddy?"

What Leonard had said made sense, but he needed time to look into it himself.

"Len, Rita's always right on the money with the numbers. You know that. You and I have been going back and forth about this for months now. I want to find out what's happening with your accounts, as much as you do…but Rita? Seriously? How can you even suggest that she has anything to do with this?"

"I'm just asking you to consider the possibility, Roy. Let's talk again soon."

As Leonard Zimmerman hung up the phone, he had a very uneasy feeling. Someone was stealing his money, and he was going to get to the bottom of it with or without Roy's help.

CHAPTER 29

Bubbe's Illness

Sarah was shaken by the recent days' events. Why didn't Jonathan or Rita want to answer her questions? She had always been so proud of her bookkeeping skills. Still, with all the things going on recently, she half wished she had never gotten involved with it, never worked at Thomas Finance Co., never gotten promoted, never took over the Zimmerman account, and never met Jonathan. He was furious with her about turning down his marriage proposal, something she hadn't shared with Bubbe. She did tell Mitzi about it, who suggested she break things off with Jonathan. To calm her nerves, she decided to walk home. It took her an additional half hour, but she needed the time to think.

As she entered the apartment, she was surprised to see her Uncle Robert sitting with David and Steven on the sofa, both of whom looked like the world had ended.

Oh no, oh no. "What's wrong? Where's Bubbe? Uncle Robert, where's Bubbe?"

"She's sick!" yelled Steven, running into his bedroom and slamming the door shut.

Sarah could hear him sobbing. Her first instinct was to go to him and help him settle down, but Uncle Robert steered her back to the sofa.

"Sarah, let him be for a while. He's upset. Bubbe had a heart attack this afternoon just after Steven returned home. He called the ambulance. He probably saved her life. She's at Beth Israel Hospital now. The crisis has passed for now, and she should be home in a week or so. Look, Sarah, Bubbe isn't getting any younger, and it's going to take her a while to recover. I've spoken to my brothers. We've agreed to chip in and pay for a nurse to come and stay with her until she's a little stronger. But we still need someone to watch over the boys. Can you take a few hours off from work, in the morning and afternoon, until we can figure out some other arrangements?"

"Whoa, I don't need taking care of," said David, throwing his hands up in the air. "I can take care of myself."

"David, enough. We're going to play by my rules now, and that includes your sister keeping tabs on you and Steven. Get it? Now sit and be quiet or go into your room."

Sarah had been watching this interchange with her uncle and David. To her great surprise, David sat back down and just stared at the rug in front of him. He had inherited their father's hair-trigger temper. She began wondering what their lives would be like if Bubbe was no longer a part of them. She couldn't. Bubbe had to be okay. She just had to be. She needed her grandmother as much, if not moreso, than the boys did.

Looking over at his niece, Robert could see she was crying. Putting his arms around her and drawing her near, he whispered in her ear that everything was going to be okay. To be honest, he wasn't sure that was the case at all. His mother was getting on in years; how much longer could she do this? He remembered holding his sister, Rose, in much the same way and telling her the same thing after the jerk she married had cheated on her. He had the same sick feeling then, that he had now, holding his niece— things weren't going to be okay. They were just going to get worse. Sarah reminded him so much of his sister, and he could only hope that she never had to go through what her mother had endured throughout her marriage. That idiot she married was responsible for all of this. He bullied Rose, neglected her when she became ill, and after she died, abandoned his children. Because of Henry's actions, his mother had to step in and take care of his sister's kids. She shouldn't have this kind of responsibility at her age. *Hell, she's eighty-seven. She should be sitting around a pool in Ft. Lauderdale or in the Catskills, right now, exchanging recipes, not in a damn hospital bed.*

***

Sarah contacted Mr. Zimmerman and requested a few hours a day off. He asked if she would take the books home with her and work on them, which she eagerly agreed to; at least it would keep her mind off Bubbe. Aunt Julie watched the boys, while Sarah stopped at the office to get the ledgers. Once back at home, she decided to delve into the numbers, but her focus was off. Every time she looked at the ledger, she saw a vision of her Bubbe in a hospital bed with tubes going in and out of her arms, nurses hovering over her, and doctors stopping by to check on her progress.

Bubbe had been in the hospital for several days. How Sarah hated hospitals. Her mother had died in one just seven years earlier. Her hospitalization lasted six weeks, the last five of which she spent in a coma. At the time, no one wanted to scare Sarah or her siblings, so neither Bubbe nor her aunts or uncles mentioned that Rose was dying. Nate may have known—he was sixteen at the time, but if he did, he kept quiet. Sarah felt as if she never got to say goodbye and tell her mother how much she loved and appreciated her. And as far as Sarah's father, Henry, was concerned, Rose's comatose state gave him license to abandon her in her greatest time of need. Sarah hated him for that and so many other things.

On the day of her mother's funeral, Henry stood at her gravesite, playing the forlorn widower, accepting condolences from friends, family, and community members. Many of them had no idea what a horrible person he was. This would be the last family event Henry attended. Although he was still in town, he didn't attend the unveiling ceremony for her mother's gravestone a year later, a Jewish tradition of memorializing the dead. He refused to pay for the marker; Sarah's uncles took care of that.

As far as Sarah was concerned, Henry was dead to her. It would only be a matter of a few years after the funeral that he chose to abandon Sarah and her siblings and moved on with his life, leaving Bubbe and her uncles to clean up the mess.

With Bubbe in the hospital, things at home had become a bit more challenging. Steven was spending less and less time with her and David and more time in his bedroom. He missed Bubbe terribly. She had been the only mother he had ever known, or at least remembered. Steven was six when Rose died. He had been through so much these last few years.

David's behavior, on the other hand, was a pleasant surprise. He was offering to help around the apartment with the household chores. Would wonders never cease? Nate was also helping, but he had such a busy schedule that much of the burden fell on Sarah, a responsibility that scared her to no end.

Within a few days, Sarah had made arrangements with a neighbor who agreed to check in on the boys until Sarah returned from work every day. On her first full day back in the office, Mr. Zimmerman invited her to step into his office and talk for a bit.

Had she done something wrong? Did Jonathan stir up any trouble while she was out? Was she going to get fired? As her fears surfaced and began shooting through her mind, Sarah could feel her heart pounding, her legs growing heavier and heavier, and her mouth becoming parched. What could Mr. Zimmerman possibly want to speak to her about? *Did he find out that Jonathan had proposed? Was he upset that she rejected him? Did Mr. Zimmerman think she was progressing too slowly with finding out who was stealing from the company? Did he think she was somehow involved?*

Sarah could feel sweat coming down from her hairline, forming tiny droplets on her forehead by the time she sat down.

"Sarah, are you okay? You look ill. Maybe you should go home for the rest of the day?"

"Um, no, no, really, I'm fine, Mr. Zimmerman. What is it you wanted to discuss?"

"If you're sure. You are a valuable employee around here, and I want to make sure you stay healthy."

Valuable? Sarah could breathe again.

"Sarah, I'm curious if you and Rita have uncovered anything else about our mystery thief?"

"Not yet, but I think we're closing in on it."

"Good. Good. I'd like you to set up a meeting with you, Rita, Jonathan, and me."

Sarah could feel that warm, sick feeling come over her again. Jonathan still wasn't speaking to her, and she was in no great hurry to tear down his wall of silence.

"Let me speak with Rita. I'm sure it won't be a problem. Do you think it's necessary for Jonathan to be at the meeting?" asked Sarah.

"I'd like him there. Is that going to be an issue? I haven't wanted to pry, but I've noticed that things have been a little icy between the two of you. Anything I need to be concerned about?"

"Certainly not, Mr. Zimmerman. Everything is under control."

CHAPTER 30

Everything Is Under Control

"**E**verything is under control?" *What was she thinking? Jonathan was never under control.*

When she returned to her desk, Sarah called Rita about the meeting. "Hi, Rita. Mr. Zimmerman would like to call a meeting with you, Jonathan, and me to discuss the problem areas in the books. When are you available? Mr. Zimmerman said any time is fine with him."

"Hon, do you think it's necessary that I be at the meeting?" asked Rita. "I mean, I'm doing you a favor, and I don't mind doing it, but I don't work for Mr. Zimmerman. You do."

Sarah wished the meeting would just go away too. "Not my choice, Rita. Mr. Zimmerman is insisting on it. Besides, he's a client of Mr. Thomas. If you won't do it for your boss, I'm asking you to do it for me as a friend. Please!"

"Okay, I'll be there. Anything to help out a friend."

Even before she set the phone receiver down, Sarah could smell his cologne. She wondered if her olfactory senses were playing games again. But when she turned around, Jonathan was standing behind her. "I just saw my uncle. I wouldn't miss this meeting, baby doll. I can't wait to tell Uncle Leonard what you've been up to."

"What?! What are you planning?"

"Wouldn't you like to know?"

The days leading up to the meeting were torture for Sarah. Jonathan kept leaving her cryptic notes, mocking her. Notes that said things like "I don't know what you and Rita are cooking up, but you're not going to get away with it." "I've been keeping tabs on you." "I can't believe my uncle let you bring Rita into this. She's not trustworthy." "You'll be sorry you said no to me. I'll make you pay for that."

Walking into Mr. Zimmerman's office on the day of the meeting, Sarah saw that Jonathan, Mr. Zimmerman, and Rita were already seated. Rita was telling Mr. Zimmerman a story about her son, Daniel.

"…and then next fall, he's hoping to attend college," said Rita, ending her story.

"You must be very proud of him, Rita," said Mr. Zimmerman.

"I am," Rita replied.

"Yeah, yeah, yeah, we're all proud of little Daniel's accomplishments," Jonathan chimed in. He was staring so intently at Sarah that he didn't even notice Rita glaring at him.

"Uncle Leonard, has Sarah told you about our big news?"

Sarah stared at Jonathan in disbelief. He couldn't possibly be planning to use this meeting to announce that she turned down his marriage proposal. She could feel her cheeks burning.

"No, she hasn't, although I've noticed some tension lately."

"Well, Sarah and I are forming a partnership. Aren't we, Sarah?"

"What kind of partnership?" Mr. Zimmerman chuckled, hoping that his nephew had the brains to propose to Sarah.

What is he doing? Not now, you meshugunah! Sarah thought. "Yes, Jonathan, what are you talking about?" Sarah asked.

Rita was looking at her oddly. Did Rita believe that she would join Jonathan in any type of venture, business or otherwise.

"Nothing that requires a contract, but she and I have been trying to figure out who has been taking money from the company, and I think we've found out who it is."

"Who!" his uncle asked, jumping up from his chair.

"Well, I've been hesitant to point fingers, but I believe Rita has a confession to make. Sarah, you really messed up here. You brought the fox right into the henhouse. You should have heeded my warnings."

"Mr. Zimmerman, I swear I don't know what Jonathan is talking about," Sarah said in an apologetic tone.

"Jonathan, are you sure about this? This is quite an accusation to make about someone," Mr. Zimmerman countered.

Sarah could see Rita was agitated. She watched her friend stand up and walk toward the door. But before she reached her destination, Mr. Zimmerman called after her, stopping Rita in her tracks. "Rita, I can't force you to stay, but I would think that you'd at least want to defend yourself."

"There is no defense to the garbage that just came out of your nephew's mouth. He's only saying that because we've been having an affair, and he's angry that I haven't been paying as much attention to him as of late."

"An affair! Rita, don't you think you're a little too old for my nephew? And what about Sarah?"

Sarah couldn't believe what she was hearing. How could this be true? Jonathan had proposed to her, and Rita was her friend. "Jonathan, I would have expected something slimy like this from you, but Rita," she said, turning to her, "you're my friend, or at least I thought you were. How could you!" Sarah ran from Mr. Zimmerman's office into the powder room.

Upon her exit, Jonathan and Rita began to bicker. "Both of you sit down now before I call the police. I'm going to check on Sarah, and neither one of you is to get out of your seats. Have I made myself clear? Before the end of today, we're going to get this mess hammered out."

Mr. Zimmerman stood awkwardly outside the woman's bathroom. He could hear her muffled cries through the door. Knocking softly, he said: "Sarah, it's Mr. Zimmerman. I don't want you to think I blame you for any of this. But as the person who first came across the missing money, I need you in on the meeting.

Sarah couldn't breathe.

"Sarah, can you hear me?"

"Yes, Mr. Zimmerman, I hear you. I need a minute. It's just been a rough few weeks."

"It's okay, Sarah. Come back to my office as soon as you can," Mr. Zimmerman said in a fatherly tone.

Reentering his office, he closed the door behind him. "Sarah needs a few moments to compose herself, and I can't blame her. Jonathan, how can you be such a cad to that sweet girl? And Rita, you should have known better. When she returns, we'll continue this meeting. Jonathan, I hope to God you have proof of what you're intimating."

"Sweet girl? When I tell you—" Jonathan's rant was cut off by his uncle.

"Enough!"

Taking the chance to jump into the conversation, Rita said, "He has nothing on me because I didn't do anything wrong! He's only trying to cover his tracks."

Mr. Zimmerman pounded his desk with his fist. "All I know is someone better start telling me the truth around here!" He stormed out again.

CHAPTER 31

The Betrayal

S arah felt ill. Her life was crumbling before her. Bubbe was sick, which was awful in and of itself. Now she had found out that Rita, whom she considered a friend and confidant, had betrayed her, and it was heartbreaking.

Before the meeting, she had shared some of the recent goings-on with Mitzi, her rock, who warned her that something didn't seem right and to watch her back with Rita. When Mitzi first said this, Sarah had laughed, asking her childhood friend when she had become became so suspicious of people. But now, she had to admit that Mitzi was right on target. Why hadn't she listened to her?

Looking from Jonathan to Rita made her blood boil. Sarah had always thought of herself as someone who was a good judge of character, but she had obviously completely misjudged Rita. She thought they were friends. How could she have been so stupid? And Jonathan; what a cad. He had proved himself to be erratic and untrustworthy. So, she felt betrayed by him too, but more so bewildered as to why he even bothered with her, in the first place, if he was already in a relationship! *But Rita?* Rita had always been there for Sarah. She had become a big sister, of sorts, always there when Sarah had a problem to discuss or good news to share.

What did Jonathan mean that Rita had a confession to make? Was the affair the confession? Or did he mean something else? With Jonathan, it could refer to any number of things. Specificity and clarity were not his strengths. Maybe Jonathan was trying to implicate Rita as the one who was embezzling company funds? That's ridiculous. Why would Rita do that? Maybe Jonathan was the one diverting the funds, and he was trying to pin it on Rita?

Sarah closed her eyes. It was all too much to comprehend.

Mr. Zimmerman was pacing from one end of the office to the other. Every time he passed Jonathan, he looked like he wanted to strangle him. Maybe that was why he continued to pace. It prevented him from putting his hands around Jonathan's neck.

Suddenly, he stopped. "We're going to stay here until I get some answers. I'm going to speak with each of you separately. Jonathan, you're going to start, and you better hope to God that I believe you. I want you to think very carefully before you speak. Sarah and Rita, I'm going to ask you both to step out into the main office until it's your turn."

Sarah walked out to her desk and slid into her chair, exhausted by what had just transpired. She heard Rita walking behind her, but there was nothing Sarah wanted to say to her.

Tapping her on the shoulder, Rita asked, "So I assume you're not going to speak to me because of what you just heard in there?"

"What am I supposed to do, Rita? You made me believe you were my friend, and then the next thing I know, you and Jonathan are having an affair, or should I say have been having an affair for a couple of years. Boy, you and he must have had a good laugh at my expense. All that time I was telling you my innermost feelings about him, you knew, you knew he didn't care for me, and you let him take advantage of me!"

Looking repentant, Rita said, "Look, it wasn't my intention to do that. At the time Jonathan and you met, he and I were taking a break from one another. You have to believe me. I was glad to see that he was interested in someone closer to his age. I've only wanted the best for him and you—honest."

Then there was silence. Rita wondered if Sarah believed her tale; at least she hoped she did. She still needed Sarah on her side.

"If this were any other time, I would have believed you without a second thought, Rita. Up until today, I trusted my gut instincts. They've rarely let me down. I don't know what to believe anymore. Do I believe that you and Jonathan duped me into having a romantic relationship with him so that you could continue on with your rendezvous? Or that you and Jonathan had broken up before he started to date me? I truly don't know what to believe. I'm tired. It's been a long day, and I just want to go home. Oops, I better call my Uncle Louie to see if he can go over and get dinner for the boys."

"Is your grandmother taking the night off?" asked Rita trying to lighten things up.

"She had a heart attack several days ago and is still hospitalized."

"Oh, Sarah, I'm so sorry to hear…"

"I don't need your sympathies, Rita. Now, please excuse me. I have to call my uncle."

Rita turned around to look into Mr. Zimmerman's office. She couldn't see Jonathan's face; his back was to her, but she could hear his voice. He was panicked.

"Looks like Jonathan is getting grilled by his uncle. Poor dear. He's never performed well under pressure."

Sarah didn't bother replying. She was disgusted by the entire situation. She turned around to call her uncle and complete some work at her desk, leaving Rita to sit and watch the goings-on in Mr. Zimmerman's office.

Twenty minutes later, the door opened. Jonathan came out with a scowl on his face, grabbed his jacket, and left. Mr. Zimmerman stood, watching from his office doorway, looking a bit haggard. "Sarah, why don't you go home? You and I can talk tomorrow. Have a good night."

As if on cue, Rita also picked herself up and started moving toward the door. "Oh no, not you, Rita. We still need to speak."

"You know what, Mr. Zimmerman. I'm no longer interested in this conversation. Whatever Jonathan told you is a figment of his imagination, and I want no part of it. I don't work for you, so I think I'll just leave with Sarah."

"Is that so? Well, you may not work for me, but you do work for Roy Thomas, and he won't be too pleased to hear what I have to tell him about you. And I'm not sure the police will take too kindly to it either. So, I suggest you reconsider your decision, and come into my office, sit down, and talk."

Sarah was so stupefied by Rita and Mr. Zimmerman's exchange that she found herself lingering at the front door for a few minutes.

"Good night, Sarah," said Mr. Zimmerman. "No need to wait for Rita. She'll be here with me for a while."

CHAPTER 32

It Has to Be Rye

S arah needed to clear her head before seeing the boys and her Uncle Louie. A nice walk to the bakery and then home was just the remedy. Her brothers would know something was wrong, and if they didn't pick up on it, her uncle certainly would. Ever since she was a little girl, Uncle Louie could sense her emotions. Her mother could do that too.

Sarah was so deep in thought about what had just transpired at the office that she absentmindedly passed the bakery. She had promised David she would pick up a loaf of rye. David wouldn't eat his sandwiches on anything but rye. He had always been a picky eater. Steven, on the other hand, would pretty much eat whatever you put in front of him.

It wasn't until she walked a full two blocks past it and saw the street sign that she noticed her error.

"Sugar." She turned around and headed back to Bamberg's bakeshop, scolding herself along the way. She was late enough because of that horrible meeting and didn't need this extra delay right now.

She braced herself as she walked in. The bakery had a bell above the doorway that clanged instead of chimed. That sound just sent shivers up her spine.

"Good evening, Sarah," said Mr. Bamberg from behind the counter. "I was just about to start closing down for the day. How can I help you?"

"I need a rye bread with caraway seeds, sliced thick, Mr. Bamberg."

"You got it. Can I interest you in any of our cookies? They're half-price at the end of the day."

"No thanks. Bubbe and I are still paying the dentist for the boys' last visit. They don't need any more sweets."

Handing her the loaf of rye, Mr. Bamberg said: "You take care of yourself. And say hello to your grandmother for me."

Sarah was about to tell Mr. Bamberg about Bubbe's recent heart attack but decided against it. She didn't want to tempt the evil eye. Kina hora. It's not that she really believed in the superstition itself, but why take any chances? She had just left Bamberg's and was about to turn the corner when she heard a car beep. It was Mr. Thomas. He rolled down the car window, leaned over and asked, "Need a ride? I'm going to pass your apartment building on the way home. Hop in."

"Thanks, Mr. Thomas. I appreciate this."

"I don't mind doing it all, Sarah. Is Zimmerman working you hard? Or do you usually work late hours these days? I guess the boys get their own dinner by now."

Mr. Thomas was just making conversation, but Sarah took a moment to answer him. Should she tell Mr. Thomas what was going on in the office? How much had Mr. Zimmerman shared with him? He was Mr. Zimmerman's accountant so maybe…

"No, I usually don't work this late, but today we had a meeting at the office. I made arrangements with Uncle Louie to get the boys dinner just in case it ran over."

"If I'm not prying, and tell me if I am, is this the meeting Zimmerman was going to have with you, Rita, and Jonathan?"

"He told you about it?"

"Well, he mentioned that you were being a great help in uncovering whoever was stealing money from his company and that you had asked Rita to help."

Oh no, Sarah didn't want to get Rita into trouble, even though she wasn't one of her favorite people right now.

"Mr. Thomas, I only asked Rita to help because she had worked on the account before I took it over. I don't want you to think that she was doing this on your time because…"

"Sarah…it's okay. I don't mind Rita helping at all. How did things go?"

"I'm not sure. A lot of things came out, making me question who my friends really are. And then Mr. Zimmerman spoke to Jonathan and Rita separately and told me I could leave."

"Huh." Thomas could sense Sarah was holding back information, but he didn't want to press the issue. She sounded exhausted. Instead, he decided to take a humorous tack. "Sounds like the basis for a good mystery book," he said grinning.

"I'm not sure about how good a novel it would make, but it certainly has been interesting so far."

"Well, here we are. I'd like to walk you in if that's okay," said Mr. Thomas, as he pulled into a parking space in front of Sarah's building.

"I'm fine really, Mr. Thomas."

"I'm going to watch until you get into the building. You can never be too careful. Let me know if you need anything. You know I'm always here for you."

"I will, Mr. Thomas. Thank you again for the ride. You won't tell Mr. Zimmerman that I mentioned the meeting, will you?"

"Not a word. It'll be our little secret."

Walking up the stairs, Sarah could hear Uncle Louie and the boys talking. As usual, David's voice could be heard above everyone else's.

Before she even had a chance to turn the knob, Steven yanked open the door. "Sarah's home. Sarah's home," he said, holding her hands while he jumped up and down.

"Why are you…? As her eyes scanned the room, Sarah saw Bubbe sitting in her chair. "Bubbe." Sarah let go of Steven's hands and ran toward her grandmother with her arms spread wide. She gave her a gentle but long hug. "Why didn't you tell me you were coming home? Uncle Louie, you should have called me."

"Shah, shah," Bubbe said as she smoothed her hand over Sarah's hair. "Ve didn't vant to bother you at vork. You've been so busy lately, and I'm fine. Don't vorry; this vill be a surprise for Nate as vell. My Louie picked me up from the hospital, and then ve met the boys here vhen they got home from school. Everything is all right."

David saw the bag of rye bread and grabbed it out of Sarah's hand.

"David! I was going put that in the kitchen," Sarah said in a teasing tone. She felt so much lighter, just knowing that Bubbe was home where she belonged.

"Not before I get the heel. It's the best part."

Everyone started to laugh. When David was younger, he would turn his nose up at the heel of bread and refuse to eat it. Bubbe would shake her finger at him, telling him it was the best part of the loaf and that she had never met a Jewish boy who didn't like the heel of the rye bread. And now he liked it! Would wonders never cease?

After the boys went to bed and Uncle Louie said his goodbyes, Sarah sat on the footstool at Bubbe's feet. "I missed you so much. I got a little taste of what it would be like without you being here, and I didn't like it one bit. Promise me, Bubbe…promise me you'll never leave me." Sarah could feel the tears filling her eyes, falling over her lashes, and streaming down to her cheeks. But before they could make their way down her chin, Bubbe had wiped them off, her fingers gently glossing over Sarah's skin as if she was trying to wipe away all of Sarah's sadness.

"Don't cry, mamala. There's enough in life to cry about vithout you vorrying about me."

Sarah loved it when her grandmother called her mamala. It was an endearment that she had used since Sarah was little. It meant little mama. Sarah had once asked Bubbe why she called her that. Her grandmother told her that she had the soul of a much older and wiser person.

Sarah was certain that Bubbe would not think she was so wise if she knew what had just happened at the office. How could she have been so naïve? As much as she wanted to talk to her grandmother about Rita and Jonathan and what was going on at work, she couldn't. Uncle Louie made her promise that Bubbe would get some peace and quiet, and Sarah was going to make certain that happened.

The Blame Game

The more Sarah thought about it, the angrier she became. It was obvious to her that Jonathan and Rita were both involved with the missing funds. *It all made sense now.*

That's why Jonathan was so gung-ho about her working at his uncle's company. He wasn't in love with her. He wanted to keep an eye on her so she would only get so far in her investigation. *And Rita!* Sarah believed she was her friend, but all along, she had been sleeping with Jonathan. *Yuck, yuck, and double yuck.* Rita must have gotten a good laugh when Jonathan started dating Sarah. Oh, and she had confided in Rita how much she liked him. *How humiliating! Rita knew it was a ploy all along.*

Sometimes I am so stupid! How could I not have seen this? I didn't want to see it. I wanted Jonathan to be my perfect match, and I ignored all the warning signs. I didn't listen to Bubbe... She's always been right in the past. Why did I ignore her now? I know why. I didn't want to believe that someone who was affectionate toward me could also be so damn evil. Bubbe saw it. She recognized those qualities because she had seen them before in Henry. Maybe that's how my parents ended up together. Rose fell for Henry's act just as I fell for Jonathan's.

She still didn't know the details of what had happened when Mr. Zimmerman had spoken to Rita and Jonathan. Maybe he'd tell her this morning.

However, when she got to work his door was closed so she sat at her desk and got to work. Mr. Zimmerman was locked away in his office, on the phone, all morning. *Who was he talking to?* She wondered. She soon put it all out of her mind, instead focusing on entering a new vendor's information into the general ledger. That's when she heard someone clearing their throat and looked up to see Mr. Zimmerman standing by her desk.

"Sarah, I need to fill you in on some information that has come to light."

"What type of information is it, Mr. Zimmerman? Is it about last night?"

"Step into my office, and I'll give you the full rundown."

She sat down in the armchair directly across from his desk and waited for Mr. Zimmerman to sit, but he didn't. He was in pacing mode.

"Sarah, I want to update you on what's going on." Mr. Zimmerman paused, shaking his head. "I had a long talk with Jonathan and Rita. They each blamed the other. Jonathan tried to implicate you, but I know you had nothing to do with this mess. I'm so angry with myself for assuming that since he was my nephew, my sister's son for goodness' sake, that he would have some kind of family loyalty. Instead, the little thief stole from me! I should have called the police. Heck, I threatened to do just that, but I'm holding off... I want to see what real evidence we can come up with, first."

Sarah listened, too afraid to say a word. Shaking his head, Mr. Zimmerman added, "Sarah, I want you to continue to look into my books on your own. Dig as deep as you can. I want to find out how much has been taken and how they did it. If you have any questions or need more information, talk to me or Roy Thomas. I trust him with my life. Between the two of you, we're going to get to the bottom of this."

"What should I do if Rita or Jonathan asks me if I'm still working on it?"

"You're going to have to find a way around it, Sarah. I need the two of them completely in the dark about this. Oh, and just so you're aware, my nephew is no longer able to make deposits to or withdrawals from any accounts connected with this business—no matter what he tells you. In fact, he's banned from the office for the time being. I may still be related to the little knucklehead, but that doesn't mean I'm going to give him free rein of my bank accounts. I'll call Thomas today to let him know you'll be in touch. He'll be tickled. He misses you."

Sarah didn't mention that she had just seen Mr. Thomas the previous evening. Walking out of her boss's office, she wondered if she was going to be able to pull it off. Lying was not one of her strengths, nor something she enjoyed doing. Bubbe always said she wore her heart on her sleeve. But this was important, and if Mr. Zimmerman wanted her to do it, she was going to give it her best shot.

CHAPTER 34

The Note

Sarah boarded the bus, said good morning to Charlie, and headed toward the back. It was crowded this morning. She squeezed her way into the long seat that ran along the rear of the bus. Her thoughts soon drifted to Nate. He had been working late this week, and when he got home, he was dead tired. However, she would see him at Shabbas dinner tonight. Nate had become more than a brother to her. He was her substitute father. She loved him so much.

Sarah wished she could stay home and help Bubbe prepare dinner, but she couldn't. She had to go to work, and recently it had become one of the last places she wanted to be. This last week was nothing short of grueling. Mr. Zimmerman was so wound up from all the recent chaos that he hardly left his office.

Aunt Pauline promised to stop by to help Bubbe with the cooking, and the boys said they would set the table. Uncle Louie would get the challah. Uncle Robert and Aunt Julie would pick up the wine. Her other aunts and uncles who usually joined them were either under the weather or out of town.

She'd have to find a way to get Nate, to herself, to fill him in on everything that had been happening at work, including what had happened between her and Jonathan. She had avoided confiding in

Nate about it until now, but she had to tell someone, and she didn't want to upset Bubbe. In a way, she felt responsible for Bubbe's heart attack. Her relationship with Jonathan had put undue stress on her grandmother. *What if it had caused the heart attack? She'd never forgive herself.*

Charlie's voice interrupted her thoughts. "Hey, Sarah isn't this yer stop? Or are you gonna take the tour with me this morning?"

Jumping out of her seat, Sarah grabbed her purse and went out the side door. When the bus pulled away, she realized she hadn't said goodbye to Charlie. *What is wrong with me lately?* she thought.

Entering the office, Sarah noticed something on her desk. It was a small white envelope, propped up against her typewriter. The outside simply read: Sarah. It was in Jonathan's handwriting. Hesitantly, she opened the envelope and then put it down without reading the note. Did she really want to know what it said? Sarah picked it up again and then put it on the side of her typewriter. She'd look at it later. Nothing Jonathan had to say to her really mattered at this point.

The day at work was uneventful. Mr. Zimmerman stopped at her desk a few times to drop off files and to check with her about some orders. He didn't mention Rita nor Jonathan and neither did Sarah.

It was three o'clock, time for Sarah to leave. She left early on Friday evenings for Shabbas, the Jewish Sabbath. Although Mr. Zimmerman wasn't an observant Jew, he was very respectful of her beliefs. "Good night, Mr. Zimmerman. I'll see you on Monday."

"Good Shabbas, Sarah."

Sarah left the envelope where she had placed it earlier. Shortly after she left, Mr. Zimmerman needed to retrieve a file, from her desk, and he noticed the white envelope with his nephew's chicken scratch on it.

Oh, hell, what is that idiot up to now? Leonard Zimmerman didn't want to pry, but maybe one little peek wouldn't hurt. Carefully removing it from the envelope, Zimmerman unfolded the note.

Sarah,

You'll be sorry you betrayed me. I'll make
sure you get everything you deserve.

*That little piece of… Did Sarah read this? No, she would have been
far too upset if she had. Maybe I'll just take it. If Sarah asks, I can always
feign ignorance.*

***

Nate, Uncle Louie, and Uncle Robert had given Bubbe strict
orders that she wasn't to lift a finger after dinner. Nate and Sarah
would clear the table and put everything away. Sarah could hear
the boys each trying to get their grandmother's attention. As she
was drying the last dish, Uncle Louie and Aunt Pauline poked their
heads into the kitchen to say good night. Uncle Robert and Aunt
Julie followed them out. Minutes later, when Sarah walked into the
living room, she found Bubbe fast asleep in her armchair. She looked
so peaceful and relaxed. Sarah was relieved. She had been worried
about her.

"Nate…Nate…Nate, let's play a game," Steven yelled into the
kitchen.

"Shhh. Bubbe's asleep. Hey, buddy, why don't you and David
go to bed? We have shul in the morning, and last week you fell asleep
during services."

"Come on… I was tired. I won't fall asleep again, I promise,"
Steven protested.

"Bed. Now. Both of you. Let's go."

"Yes, sir," David said, rolling his eyes and giving Nate a salute,
before heading to his room. Steven giggled and kissed Nate and Sarah
good night.

"Thanks for getting them off to bed, Nate. It's not that easy to
get them to listen to me."

"I don't mind. I know how young boys can be. Heck, it wasn't
that long ago that I was one. By the way, how is your beau? What was
his name again? Jonathan?"

"We're not seeing each other any longer."

"Why not? You were so sweet on him… Did he hurt you? Because if he hurt you…"

"Nate, we have to talk."

"Okay, let's do it now then," Nate said, holding onto his sister's hand.

***

"What did he do, Sarah?"

"He proposed."

"Marriage?" asked Nate.

"I suppose I wasn't as gracious as I could have been. But honestly, Nate, I couldn't believe after all his antics that he thought I would marry him. He was so angry with me that he left the restaurant, and I had to contact Mr. Thomas for a ride home and to pay the bill. He said he was going to have his uncle fire me and that he'd make me pay for it."

"I'll kill him!" Nate said in a hushed voice, not wanting to wake his grandmother. "Who does this creep think he is leaving you like that without even paying the bill?"

"Calm down and listen. I blamed myself at first…until I found out the truth."

"The truth?"

"Oh, Nate, so much has happened; you just wouldn't believe it. With everything else going on, there has been money missing from the Zimmerman accounts. Mr. Zimmerman asked me to investigate months ago. In fact, that's one of the reasons he hired me. I had found the error in his general ledger when I still worked for Mr. Thomas. Mr. Zimmerman was impressed with my work, and on Jonathan's urging, he hired me. Jonathan kept telling me that he needed me working with him because he was so in love with me. I wasn't convinced at first, but then I realized what a great opportunity it was for me. I mean I didn't go to college like some of my friends have or have a parent who owns a business. I have to take every advantage I can to get ahead."

"Sarah, come on, you're smart, pretty, a go-getter...don't put yourself down."

"I'm not putting myself down. I'm being realistic. Anyway, things came to a head several weeks ago. I received permission from Mr. Zimmerman to bring Rita in to help me find the source of the missing money, since she worked on the account before me. You remember Rita, don't you?"

"Yeah, I think I met her last year. Nice lady."

"That's what I thought. Rita and I worked on the account together for a couple of weeks, and then Mr. Zimmerman requested a meeting with Jonathan, me, and Rita. He wanted to see if we could figure out what was going on, you know, with the accounts. The meeting didn't go quite the way I expected it would."

"Let me guess. Lover boy tried to blame it on you," Nate said laughing. "You're not laughing, Sarah. That was a joke."

"Well...he did try to blame me, not for taking the money, but for not heeding his advice."

"He gave you advice about this?"

"No! But that's what he tried to convince his uncle of. He said he warned me that Rita was involved in the embezzlement and that I messed up by bringing her into it. I told Mr. Zimmerman that wasn't true."

"Did he believe you?"

"Yes. He did. He's a very nice man. But that wasn't the worst part. The worst part was Rita admitting that she and Jonathan had been having an affair for the last two years. An affair! I was devastated, Nate. She was my friend, or at least she was supposed to be my friend."

"You mean that creep dated you while he was sleeping with her? Wait a minute. Didn't you say he proposed to you! How could he ask you to marry him when he was with her? That little..."

"Shhh. You're going to wake, Bubbe. Now listen to me. I haven't spoken to either of them since that meeting. Mr. Zimmerman has asked me to continue with my investigation. He called Mr. Thomas and asked that he answer any questions I may have. I feel a little better with Mr. Thomas being there to help me. Well, I think that brings you up to date."

"I'll have to remember to catch up with you more often," Nate said, shaking his head. "Does Bubbe know?"

"No, and I feel terrible about it. I just couldn't share this with her. She expressed her concerns about Jonathan to me early on. She didn't like him and felt his behavior was similar to Henry's.

"From what you tell me, it was damn near close!"

"Shhh. Don't wake Bubbe. If she hears you swear on Shabbas, she'll have a fit. I now realize he was just like Henry, but I wasn't ready to hear it. I wasn't ready to admit that I would choose the same type of man that my mother did. I know better!"

"Sarah, don't be so hard on yourself. There are a lot of great guys out there who would love being with you. You just haven't met him yet. Forget about that jackass…"

"Nathan Judah Steinman! Did I hear you curse on Shabbas?" Bubbe was awake. "Answer me. Did you just…"

Walking over to the armchair, Nate bent down and kissed Bubbe on her forehead. "You should go to bed, Bubbe. It's late," he said.

"Don't change the subject on me, Mr. Grown-up. And you shouldn't be using those vords in front of your sister either."

"How much did you hear, Bubbe?" Sarah asked her grandmother. "Hear? Vhat vould I have heard? I'm tired, and I'm going to bed. You should too. Ve have shul in the morning."

Nate looked over to Sarah and winked. "Okay, kiddo, I'll see you in the morning."

CHAPTER 35

Shul

From her vantage point, in the balcony, at the Chevra Tillum synagogue, Sarah could see Nate sitting with the boys and her uncles in the second row of seats near the bima, where the rabbi was positioned during services. The sanctuary had been built in the round, giving her a panoramic view of the men sitting below. She watched during certain parts of the service when the congregation stood to pray. The men and post-bar mitzvah boys would adjust their tallit, prayer shawls that Jewish men wear in the synagogue, and begin to doven. It was hypnotic to watch them sway back and forth. To Sarah, it looked like white sheets blowing in the gentle wind on a spring day. They looked so peaceful.

Sitting with Bubbe and her aunts in the balcony was a little different. Her aunts would chatter away until her grandmother shushed them all. Bubbe and Sarah were following the service. She wondered what it would be like to sit with the men and be so close to the rabbi and the Torah scrolls. As a woman in an Orthodox shul, she would never be able to find out. Men and women were separated during prayer. The theory was that women would distract men from worshipping. Maybe the rabbis who decided this were married to women like her aunts and the other chatterboxes in the balcony. Sarah just wanted to pray, that's all. It didn't seem fair. She could read Hebrew as well as or better than any of her brothers.

Suddenly, she felt Bubbe's elbow in her side. "Mamala, stand up," her grandmother said in a hushed tone. "They are opening the ark." The ark held the Torah scrolls, and the congregation always stood when it was opened and the scrolls were removed.

"Sorry, Bubbe, I was daydreaming again." Bubbe had that I-know-what-you-are-thinking glimmer in her eyes. *What did she know?*

After services, there was a kiddush (refreshments), usually sponsored by a congregant. It began with a prayer over the wine and bread and expanded into snack time or lunch depending on what was on the menu for that week. After blessing the Challah, everyone would break off a piece to nosh on. And with services starting at 7:00 a.m. and lasting until 1:00 p.m. or later, sustenance was a requirement. Walking back to the apartment following services, Bubbe let Nate, David, and Steven get ahead of them. She grabbed her granddaughter's arm, intertwining it with her own to slow her down. "Sarah, have I mentioned how proud I am of you? I know I don't say it often enough, but I don't know how I vould handle the boys or our finances vithout you. I once told Jonathan that you vere a family treasure. I vasn't telling tales—in my eyes, you vill always be precious."

Sarah noticed a single tear trickle down Bubbe's cheek, as her grandmother and she continued to walk arm in arm. "Bubbe, you only think I'm a treasure because you're my grandmother, and I love you for that, but I don't think I carry as much weight with everyone else as you give me credit for."

"Nonsense. Don't let people like Jonathan or Rita or anyone else make you feel less vorthy than you are."

"Bubbe, I'm curious. I know I've told you some of the tensions between me and Jonathan and that you don't like him, but why would you lump Rita into that? I haven't mentioned her to you recently. Oh, Bubbe," said Sarah, putting her hand over her mouth, "you fibbed to me and Nate when you said you were asleep last night. You heard everything!"

"I don't know what you're talking about, Sarah. Nate…Nate… boys, wait up for us!" Her grandmother picked up her pace, rushing toward her grandsons.

CHAPTER 36

Back to Square One

When Sarah arrived at the bus stop on Monday morning, she noticed that the line was shorter than usual. Maybe that meant she wouldn't have to squeeze into the back of the bus. She hated not having any elbow or legroom.

It had started to rain, and Sarah opened her purse to retrieve her rain bonnet. Inside she saw an envelope addressed to her.

For a moment, she lost her ability to breathe, thinking that it might be from Jonathan. She wondered how he had gotten into her purse, but after looking at the handwriting, she realized it was a note from Nate.

"Sis, I want to continue our talk. I'm still deciding if I need to reconfigure Jonathan's face or not. Your big lug of a brother, Nate."

When she arrived at work, her desk phone was ringing. Lifting the receiver, to her great relief, she heard Mr. Thomas's voice.

"Sarah, I was wondering if you had time to stop by the office so we can review the Zimmerman account again. I think I may have found something interesting."

"Sure. I can be there about 5:30 this evening. Will that work?"

"Sure does, kiddo. See you later today."

As Sarah walked toward her desk, she saw Mr. Zimmerman speaking with Jonathan in his office.

She began reviewing the numbers from the tally sheets she had worked on last week, checking it over before giving it to Mr. Zimmerman. Everything balanced out to the penny. She loved it when this happened. It reminded her that she really was good at her job. It was one thing she could still feel confident in, amongst so much uncertainty, right now.

Sarah looked up to see Mr. Zimmerman standing in front of her desk. "Sarah, can we talk in my office?"

"Sure. I'll be there in a few seconds, Mr. Zimmerman."

Closing the door behind her, Sarah sat down on Mr. Zimmerman's overstuffed armchair. Mr. Zimmerman began looking through a pile of files on his desk, speeding through them as if he was watching a movie through a mutoscope machine.

"Can I help you find something, Mr. Zimmerman? You know I'm pretty good at finding things."

"Yes, you are Sarah, and that's why what I'm about to say is so difficult for me."

"Oh," she could hardly breathe.

"Sarah, you have been an exemplary employee. I couldn't have asked for anyone who was more conscientious and loyal. If it were totally up to me, we wouldn't even be having this conversation, but it's not. You see, the other morning, I told my nephew to pack his bags and get out of my company. The sniveling weasel twisted what happened and told my sister, who believes her child would never do any wrong.

"I don't understand, Mr. Zimmerman, what..."

"I'm getting to that. You see, I ran into some financial problems years ago, and my sister and her now deceased husband loaned me a substantial amount of money. Instead of having me repay the loan, they asked for partial ownership, of the firm, as silent partners. I didn't think much of it at the time. I needed the money, and they had it. They promised not to interfere in the business end of things, and they haven't, well, until now. The bottom line, it seems, is that I can't fire Jonathan." Mr. Zimmerman stopped momentarily to wipe the beads of sweat from his forehead with his handkerchief. "Look, this is killing me, but Jonathan is here to stay or at least until I can prove that he is stealing from me. My sister is demanding that I not only take Jonathan back, but that I…I…f-f-fire you. That's why you saw my nephew. He came to gloat about how much control he has over my business."

Leaning back in his chair, as if all the energy had drained from his body, he said, "I don't know what else to say, Sarah. I have to let you go. Don't worry about anything. I'm paying you through the end of the month. If you need any references at all, I'll be more than happy to give you one. Take all the time you need to pack up."

Sarah had stopped listening after hearing, "I have to let you go." Those six little words were like a dagger in her heart. She had worked so hard. She knew Jonathan was punishing her for pursuing the investigation and for turning down his proposal. *What was she going to do now?*

On the bright side, she was going to see Mr. Thomas in a couple of hours. Maybe he would have some advice for her.

***

Sarah, come in, come in," Mr. Thomas said as he opened the office door for her. "You're a bit early. Let me just get some paperwork out of the way, and then we can have our meeting. Why don't you just sit at your old desk. You remember where it is, don't you?"

Sarah knew Mr. Thomas was joking, but she was just such a bundle of nerves. Tears filled her eyes, brimming over her lower lid and down her face. Mr. Thomas looked perplexed.

"I was joking. You know that, don't you? It's really nothing to cry over," he said as he walked to Sarah and put his arm around her shoulders. "Sarah, you're shaking. What's wrong? It can't be because I told you to sit at your old desk. Here, take my handkerchief."

"Oh, Mr. Thomas, so much is happening," she said as she looked around the office to see if anyone else was there.

"Rita's left for the day, if that's what you're concerned about. She had a personal matter to address."

"I'll just bet she did," muttered Sarah.

"So, what's going on, Sarah? Why the tears? Did Jonathan say anything to you?"

"Not directly, Mr. Thomas. You said you had work to clear up. Why don't you finish that up, and I'll just wait here for you and then we can talk."

"No, young lady. You're upset, and we're going to get to the bottom of it right now."

"Mr. Zimmerman had to fire me today...and..."

"He had to what?" Mr. Thomas gasped.

"He said that he was told by his sister, who has a financial interest in his company, that he couldn't fire Jonathan like he wanted to and that instead he had to fire me."

"We'll just see about that," said Mr. Thomas as he walked toward his office and closed the door.

Although his door was shut, Mr. Thomas was speaking loudly, so Sarah could easily make out parts of the conversation.

"What the hell is going on there, Zimmerman? Sarah's in my office right now crying her eyes out because you fired her today. Would you like to explain that to me? The last time I checked, I was still your accountant. Were you planning on telling me anything about this?"

Sarah couldn't hear Mr. Zimmerman's response, but Mr. Thomas didn't look too pleased with it.

After hanging up the phone, Mr. Thomas opened his office door, beckoning Sarah with his hand to come and join him. Once inside he gave her a hug and told her not to worry about anything. "Why don't you go home Sarah, and we can meet tomorrow?"

"I don't want to go home yet. What am I going to tell Bubbe and the boys?"

"You tell them that you were such an invaluable employee that I stole you back from Zimmerman."

Sarah didn't know how to respond. This was more than she had hoped for. "Mr. Thomas, you don't have to do that. I'll find a new job."

"You don't need to look for one, Sarah. I'm dead serious. You start working for me tomorrow morning. See you at 8:00 a.m."

What about Rita? How will she respond to my working here again? she wondered.

As if he could read her mind, Mr. Thomas said, "And don't worry about Rita. If she says anything to you, let me know."

CHAPTER 37

Sarah's Back

Sarah hadn't mentioned anything to Bubbe or the boys when she returned home. Not only did she not quite know how to broach the conversation, but she also wanted to wait to see how things worked out at Mr. Thomas's. She didn't want to be a disappointment two times in a row. Could she really do this? *Work for Mr. Thomas again...with Rita?*

The next morning, she reached the office just before 8:00 a.m. Staring through the clear glass door, she saw Rita at her desk and caught a glimpse of Mr. Thomas. *This was going to be awkward.* Taking a deep breath, she pushed the door open and heard herself say, "Hi, Rita. How are you?"

Rita seemed just as surprised as Sarah that those words came out her mouth.

"Sarah...how...are...you? Do you have an appointment with Mr. Thomas? I'm sure you haven't come here to see me."

Sarah was unsure how to respond, but Mr. Thomas saved the day, or at least it appeared so at first.

"Sarah, so glad you're back. Your old desk is waiting for you. Rita, I haven't had a chance to tell you yet. Sarah is rejoining our team. I know you two have a lot to catch up on, so I'll just get back to my office. Sarah, why don't you give me a few moments and then come to see me?" he added, sprinting to his office.

What was he thinking? What was she supposed to say to Rita? Mr. Thomas knew what had happened. She had told him! Why was he doing this?

"Sarah you're going to be working here again, huh? Don't you think that will be a bit awkward considering all that has transpired these last couple of weeks? You might reconsider Mr. Thomas's offer. He was probably trying to be kind after Mr. Zimmerman canned you."

Sarah could feel her face heating up and turning red. "Who said Mr. Zimmerman let me go?"

"I have my connections, dear," Rita said, smirking. "Jonathan couldn't wait to call and tell me all the juicy details. I guess right doesn't always triumph, does it, Sarah? As far as I'm concerned, you deserve everything you have coming to you. You put your nose where you shouldn't have."

"Oh, so you're admitting that you and Jonathan did something wrong. I was under the impression that you both were claiming ignorance over the matter of the missing funds, blaming one another for the problem. Why are you still defending Jonathan? He's turned his back on you, and yet you still go back for more. What a minute… you really do love him."

Glaring at her, Rita looked as if she had just eaten something sour. Her nose crinkled up, and her lips puckered. She stormed off to the powder room.

Sarah took the opportunity to stop by Mr. Thomas's office. He could see the anger on her face. He wasn't surprised. He had just put Sarah in a rather comprising position, but it was something that had to be done. He needed to make Rita's world a little more unsettled, and bringing Sarah back into the office did the trick. Not that his job offer to Sarah wasn't genuine. It was. But if he was able to use it to get Rita back in line, then all the better.

As she entered his office and sat down on the couch, he could tell she was boiling mad. "It looks like you and Rita had a nice reunion." *That was it. How could he?* Trying to steady her nerves and respond as calmly as possible she replied, "Nice…not exactly the way I'd describe what just occurred between us. I call it more of a sparring match. I just don't understand, Mr. Thomas. You've always been so wonderful to me, and believe me, I appreciate all you have done. I really do…but how could you put me in that position?"

"What position is that, Sarah?" Thomas knew exactly what he had done, but he couldn't tell Sarah that. "I apologize if leaving you with Rita was awkward. I know what happened, and I want you to feel comfortable here. Would you like me to speak with Rita about her behavior?"

"No…it's just… I don't know. Look, we'll work it out, Mr. Thomas. I'm a big girl, and I can handle this on my own. What would you like me to start on?"

"That's the spirit, Sarah. Let's start with the Dreyfus account."

"Dreyfus…I'm not sure I'm familiar with…" she sputtered.

"Yes…yes…sorry. He's a new client. He has several manufacturing plants, and I need you to start going through all the files he provided to me and enter the numbers in the general ledger. If you have any questions at all, let me know."

Sarah left her boss's office wondering what he was up to. Something was going on. She could feel it in her bones.

That night after dinner, Sarah told Bubbe about all that had transpired over the last day and a half. How Jonathan had been so horrible to her. How Mr. Zimmerman had fired her, albeit under pressure from his sister, and how Mr. Thomas came to the rescue and hired her back. And most of all, how grateful she was to Mr. Thomas even though it meant working with Rita again. Sarah thought Bubbe would be full of questions, but instead, she kissed the top of her granddaughter's head, told her how proud she was of her, and wished her good night.

***

The next morning, Rita called in sick. Roy Thomas smiled to himself, wondering if Sarah's return had set her that off-kilter. Rita had really disappointed him. He had trusted her with so many of his larger accounts. How many others had she stuck her sticky fingers into? In the end, Leonard Zimmerman firing Sarah was a good thing. That meant that he could have a trusted employee once again. It would keep Rita on her toes at the same time. *But what to do about Rita?*

So far Leonard, Sarah, and he knew that money had been siphoned out of Zimmerman's accounts into fraudulent companies and accounts in Daniel's name. They just didn't know which of Zimmerman's accounts were real and which weren't. Jonathan wasn't sophisticated enough to pull this ploy off by himself. He needed Rita. She had the bookkeeping background and likely understood how to set up the fake companies. Jonathan had probably been the one to transfer the money as he had access to Zimmerman's books, banking information, and had the authority to make deposits and transfers. The problem was this was speculation on their part. They couldn't prove it...yet. He and Zimmerman had to find where the plan started to derail. Maybe Sarah had found something but didn't realize the significance of it. When she came back from lunch, he'd sit her down for a brainstorming session.

Just as she opened the door, Sarah saw Mr. Thomas peek his head out of his office.

"Sarah, why don't you put your things down and come in here? I thought since Rita wasn't here today, it would be a good time to review what we know about the missing Zimmerman funds.

"Sure, Mr. Thomas. I'll be right there."

As soon as she sat down across from Mr. Thomas, he got up from his desk and started pacing as he spoke. He was almost as fidgety as Mr. Zimmerman had been several days ago.

"I want to review what we know so far about the debacle at Zimmerman Co. First, we know that funds are missing from Zimmerman's main accounts. The money is coming in from vendors, but the deposits don't reflect the income. So, where's the snag? We also know that Jonathan and Rita are somehow involved in this, but how? Sarah, when you were working for Zimmerman, did you notice anything in the invoices or deposits that may have made you raise an eyebrow?"

"Actually, there was something, now that you mention it. When I first started working for Mr. Zimmerman, he asked me to check some of the accounts for him. I noticed several entries for checks, in varying amounts, to a vendor—initialed by Jonathan and made out to a Daniel Polansky. Isn't that odd?"

"Why? Who's this Daniel Polan…is that Rita's son?"

"I didn't know at the time. I told Mr. Zimmerman, and when he asked Jonathan about it, Jonathan did not take it well. I recently asked Rita about it, and she tried to brush it off."

Thomas stood, scratching his chin. "Daniel…huh? Why would that little sleazeball be making checks out to Rita's son? He's not even an adult."

"What are you going to do, Mr. Thomas?"

"I think Rita and I are going to have a little chat when she comes back into the office. In fact, I'll call her now to make sure she's coming in. Sarah, why don't you take tomorrow off on me? Spend some time with your grandmother."

"Are you sure?"

"There are few things I'm certain of in this life, Sarah, but your spending time with your grandmother and my having a heart-to-heart talk with Rita are two I feel quite strongly about. Enjoy your day off."

Sarah worked the rest of the day, wrapping up as much of the work as she could on the Dreyfus account. She had begun to warm up to the idea of having a day off and couldn't wait to tell Bubbe. Ever since her grandmother had come home from the hospital, she had wanted to spend more time with her, and this was her chance.

***

"Bubbe, Bubbe," Sarah said after closing the apartment door behind her.

"I'm in here, mamala."

Her grandmother was sitting in her armchair.

"Bubbe, you won't believe it. Mr. Thomas gave me the day off tomorrow. We can spend the entire day together."

"Is everything okay? I know Mr. Thomas likes you, but you just started to vork for him again. Vhy vould he give you a day off… now?"

"You know that I'm still working on trying to find out who embezzled from Mr. Zimmerman. Mr. Thomas and I were talking about it today, and I remembered seeing something in the books… checks with Jonathan's signature made out to the same individual and various companies. Well, I told Mr. Thomas that I had informed Mr. Zimmerman of this and that he had taken it up with Jonathan."

"And…" Bubbe asked, sitting on the edge of the chair.

"And, I found it odd that these particular payments weren't made to a company but to Daniel Polansky, Rita's son."

"Isn't he still in high school?"

"He is, Bubbe. He's graduating this year. He's never worked for the Zimmerman Company per se, but he has done some odds and ends for Jonathan, at least according to Rita. But I don't understand how small jobs would amount to payments totaling twelve thousand dollars."

"Oy gevalt. That's a lot of money, Sarah."

"I know, but the best part of this all is that I get to spend tomorrow with you."

"I'm happy too, mamala."

CHAPTER 38

All About Rose

Bubbe peeked her head into the crack of Sarah's bedroom door at 9:00 a.m. Sarah was awake but still snuggled under the covers. She was enjoying not having to leave the comfort of her bed.

"Mamala, it's nine o'clock in the morning. The sun has been out for hours, and you're not up yet. I thought ve vere going to spend the day together."

Sarah sat up and smiled at her grandmother. How can she be so chipper in the morning? She was eighty-seven, had four grandchildren who lived with her, including two very active boys. Sarah could only hope that she would be as vivacious as her Bubbe at that age. She stretched her arms wide and yawned.

"I'm getting up now, Bubbe."

"Good. I'll reheat your breakfast so it von't be stone-cold vhen you go to eat it."

Sarah walked into the kitchen just as her breakfast plate was coming out of the oven. What would she do without Bubbe? She knew she'd have to figure it out one day, but for now she was just going to enjoy her company.

"What would you like to do today? We can take the bus downtown and do a little shopping. Or I hear there's a new movie at the Capital Theater. Or we could…"

"You know vhat I'd really like to do, Sarah? I'd like to catch you up on some family history. I told you a vhile ago that I vanted to talk to you about your mother, and today is the perfect day to do it. Then after ve talk, vhy don't ve go and see vhat's playing at the Capital Theater? Deal?"

"Deal." Sarah hoped she could make it through the story this time.

Bubbe took a deep breath and began relaying the story of her daughter, Rose.

"Your mother vas our little princess. Although she vasn't my youngest child, she vas my only daughter. Your uncles gave her a hard time vhen she vas younger, alvays teasing her, asking her to do their laundry and clean their rooms. Rose vas good-natured, and so she didn't turn them down that often.

"At the same time, the boys vere very protective of her. One time, vhen Rose was in the fifth grade, a boy in her class started to bully her. Vhen my boys found out, they beat up the boy. I remember getting the phone call from the school telling me that my ragamuffins vere causing trouble again. I vas upset about the call, but I also knew that the boys didn't go around picking fights. It vasn't until ve returned home that Louie spoke up and told me that they vere only protecting Rose. He said they had told the principal that too, but she didn't believe them. After Rose confirmed Louie's story, I vent the next day to the school vith a neighbor who spoke better English than me. I demanded that the child who bullied Rose apologize, and I had a discussion vith his parents. I don't know vhat his parents said to him, but he never bothered your mother again. Rose grew up around boys and men who vere protective of her." It was at this point that Bubbe took a deep breath. Her next words came out choked, as tears started to puddle in her eyes.

"As Rose got older and started dating, she dated some very nice young men from good Jewish families. Your grandfather, Lazar, kept telling me she vas going to marry Sam Singer. His family vent to our synagogue. I thought so, too, until…" Bubbe stopped speaking and sat down in her armchair.

"Until what, Bubbe? What happened to Sam? Why didn't my mother marry him?"

"Sam met someone else, and he dropped Rose. On the outside, she seemed fine, but I knew she vas falling apart inside. You see, the girl who he left Rose for vas her best friend, Miriam. She not only lost her love. She lost the closest friend she had ever had. After that, Rose didn't date, nor did she go out very much at all. Your uncles vere vorried about her and talked her into going to a dance at our synagogue one night. Your mother looked so beautiful that evening. She vore a midnight blue dress. I loaned her my pearl necklace. She looked like a princess...I remember it like it vas yesterday," Bubbe's voice trailed off.

"And...and...come on, Bubbe, what happened at the dance?"

"That night your mother came home beaming. She told me she had met a vonderful young man. He was new to our community, having grown up in Washington, D.C. She assured me he came from a good Jewish family. When I asked the boys about him, they vere less enthusiastic. They said he seemed to be polite, but there vas something about him that bothered them, something they couldn't put their finger on. I laughed and told them to stop being so over-protective of their little sister. I still regret that. I should have listened to them."

Bubbe was quite for a moment, lost in her memories.

"The following day, there vas a knock at the door. Vhen I answered it, a handsome young man vas standing on the porch. I didn't open the door and invite him in because Lazar vas still at vork, and I didn't know this young man from Adam. He vas extremely polite, introduced himself to me as Henry Steinman, and apologized for not calling beforehand. He told me that he had met Rose the evening before. He vanted to ask her father and me if he could take her out on a date. I invited him to come back that evening and have tea and cake with us. Vhen your mother heard he vas coming over, she vas beside herself. She started lamenting about having nothing to vear, asking me how I could spring this on her and if I thought her father vould approve. Oy...if I knew she vas going to carry on like that I vould have told him to go avay...probably vhat I should have done...but I didn't."

"That evening, Henry told us a good story. He said he vas a partner at a grocer's that had opened in our neighborhood recently. That he vas very close vith his family. That he vas a hard vorker. I didn't even think of questioning him. I believed him!"

"After they had started dating, things slowly unraveled. Ve discovered that Henry vasn't a partner but that he vorked as a clerk for the store. He never mentioned his family and from vhat your grandfather and I could tell 'hard vork' vas not in his vocabulary."

Sarah sat with her mouth agape.

"Sarah, I'm not telling you this to denigrate your father but to show you that there vere signs from the very beginning of their relationship that your mother ignored. When I told Rose that her father and I veren't comfortable vith Henry's lies and that ve thought it best that she break up vith him, she refused. She told us that ve didn't understand how much Henry meant to her…how sveet he vas…how much hurt he had been through in his life…and how ve should be embracing him vith love and not turning him avay. After our talk, I felt bad and questioned vhether Lazar and I vere being fair vith the young man."

Bubbe stood up once more, wiped her palms on her dress, and walked into the kitchen. "I'm getting a bisl tea."

Sarah knew what that meant. Every time her grandmother had to discuss something unpleasant, she'd brew some tea. It settled her nerves.

"May I have a cup of tea too, Bubbe?"

As Bubbe placed the glasses of hot tea on the kitchen table, she continued reminiscing about Rose and Henry.

"After Rose arrived home one evening, from a date with Henry, I noticed bruises on her upper arms. I asked her about it. She started crying and told me that Henry had gotten upset vith her and latched onto her upper arms and started shaking her. She vas terrified. I vas furious. Rose begged me not to tell Lazar.

"Sarah, that vas the first time I didn't confide in your grandfather, and to this day, I regret it. I sat up for hours that night trying to convince your mother to break things off vith Henry. She just sat there shaking her head from side-to-side with tears streaming down her cheeks. Through her tears, she kept saying, 'I can't leave him; I just can't. It's my fault. I shouldn't have upset him. It's my fault.' No matter vhat I said to console her, she vouldn't listen. The relationship continued. I didn't see any other signs that he vas touching her, but I knew if he vasn't hitting her, he vas intimidating her. Either vay it vas vrong…"

Sarah sat with tears rolling down her face, not knowing what to say.

"Your mother continued to date him. I suspected Henry vas still manhandling her, but Rose vas careful to cover up any evidence of that. Then one day, your mother came home vith a ring on her finger. I couldn't believe my eyes. You mother just looked at me and said, 'Congratulate me. Henry proposed, and I said yes.' Henry didn't ask your grandfather for your mother's hand in marriage. It just isn't the vay things are done!"

"Vhen your grandfather came home from vork that day, I told him about the engagement, and updated him on my suspicions about Henry being rough vith your mother. He and I had a long discussion vith Rose that evening and forbade her to marry him. She ran from the house saying she didn't care vhat ve thought. Later that night, when she came home, she vouldn't even speak to us. I vas heartbroken. The boys tried talking to her, but she started yelling, accusing them of taking my side and not caring about her happiness. "Lazar and I decided ve didn't vant to lose our daughter over this, so ve chose to keep our opinions to ourselves. Lazar had a heart-to-heart talk vith Henry, who denied ever touching Rose, another lie.

"Vithin six months, your mother vas married to Henry. Your grandfather and I paid for the vedding. It vas a small affair. But vhat struck me as odd vas that no one from his family attended, not his parents nor his siblings. Everyone at that vedding vas from our family."

All the time her grandmother was speaking, Sarah was sipping her tea, wondering if she could listen any longer. "Bubbe, if this is too much for you, we can talk another time. I don't want to upset you any more than I already have."

"No, no, you have a right to know, and since your mother is no longer around to tell you, I vill."

***

Bubbe continued with her story. "At first, the marriage seemed to be going vell, and Lazar and I breathed a bit more easily. Rose appeared happy, and there veren't any further signs that Henry had become violent vith her. I began to think that Lazar's talk vith him had had an effect. Your mother told me that Henry vaited on her hand and foot. I doubted that, but as long as your mother vas happy, your grandfather and I vere happy. It vas about six months into the marriage that I started to notice a difference in Rose, a sadness in her eyes.

"I stopped by Henry and Rose's apartment one day to find out more. Vhen I got there, Rose vas in tears. Henry has been missing dinners, coming home all hours of the night."

"Where was he going?" Sarah asked.

"Your mother asked him, but he became very defensive and mean. Rose vas too scared to take the conversation further. That's vhen your uncles decided to take things into their own hands. One night, Frank and Jake vaited near the store vhere Henry vorked and followed him. He didn't go home. He vent to an apartment building for vhich he had a key. They couldn't get in, so they didn't know vhich apartment he vent to or who he vent to see. They vaited outside to see vhat vould happen. In an hour and a half, Henry emerged vith a brunette hanging on his arm. They looked very cozy together, and Henry gave her a long goodbye kiss."

"Then they followed him home. They decided not to confront Henry, not that night at least. They knew the only vay to convince Rose to leave him vas to show her that his behavior vas not a once-in-a-vhile occurrence but a pattern."

"They followed him from vork to the brunette's apartment several times more. Henry had established a routine. Your uncles planned to sit Rose down the following week vhile Henry vas at vork.

Maybe they could convince her to leave the mamzer before he came home that night."

"Bubbe! You swore."

"I'm trying to be as honest as I can. The next morning, before they even had a chance to speak vith her, Rose called them. She claimed she had fallen down the stairs the night before and needed them to take her to the hospital. She said she vould have asked Henry to take her, but he had to leave for vork early."

Sarah got up and hugged her grandmother. "Bubbe this is… tearing me up. I knew Henry was horrible, but this…this is too much for one day. Can we continue this talk another time?"

"Ve never have to speak of this again, mamala. I needed to tell you at least this much so you vould understand vhy I had such an instant dislike to Jonathan. I vant you to know how proud I am of you. You are a much better judge of character than your mother vas. You saw right through that schmendrik. One day, you're going to meet a vonderful man who is going to cherish you and treat you like a queen because that is vhat you deserve."

"I love you, Bubbe. Thank you for sharing my mother's story with me. I'll tell you what. I'm going to get washed up, and then we'll see what's playing at the Capital. I'm in the mood for a good comedy."

Watching Sarah leave the kitchen, Molly felt a burden had been lifted, one she had carried around for years. Being able to tell Sarah about Rose and Henry was a relief. She also came to understand that she had been unfair to her granddaughter, assuming that because she was Rose's daughter, she would make the same mistakes her mother had. Sarah, Molly realized, was her own very special person.

CHAPTER 39

Where's Rita?

Having a day off was nice, but Sarah had heard enough about the horrible manner in which her father treated her mother to last a lifetime.

Arriving at work the next morning, she was met with a floral delivery. She hadn't received flowers since Mr. Zimmerman sent them to her for finding the almost-certain embezzlement. She couldn't stop smiling. The flowers were from Nate, with a note that read, "Always remember, you're one strong cookie. Love, Nate."

Looking up, she saw Mr. Thomas standing at her desk with a concerned look on his face. "Mr. Thomas, did you need anything?"

"No. I saw the flowers, and I thought Jonathan might be on the prowl again."

"Don't worry. He no longer has a reason to romance me. This is from my brother, Nate. He wanted to remind me of how strong I am."

"He sounds like he's a great big brother. By the way, Sarah, how was your day off?"

"Nate's a mensch. He always has been. As for my day off with my grandmother, we had a nice heart-to-heart talk. Did you speak with Rita, Mr. Thomas?"

"Yes, Sarah, I surely did."

"By the way, where is Rita this morning?" Before her boss could answer, she added, "Huh, I don't think I've ever seen her desk so neat, Mr. Thomas, have you?"

"No, you're right about that, Sarah. It's never been that neat. But I can guarantee it will be that way, at least, for a while."

Noticing the quizzical look on Sarah's face, he added, "You see, Rita and I touched upon several topics, including her position at this firm. Do you remember signing an agreement that you would be discreet with our clients' accounts and maintain the highest ethical standards in your work?"

"Yes, I do. I told you at the time that I would sign it, but it wasn't necessary because I would never do anything that would hurt or embarrass you…oh…"

"Exactly. Well, Rita signed that same agreement. She promised to uphold the ethical standards that I had set for my practice. When I brought it up to her, she demanded to see the paper, noting that it probably wasn't even her signature. When I produced the paperwork, she grabbed it from the file, tore it up and then threw it in my face. After she grabbed her things, she left! Luckily, I guessed right about how Rita would react to the confrontation. The document she had torn up was a carbon copy and not the original. I'm going to let her brood about it for a few days. That will give you and I some time to look deeper into the account with Daniel Polansky's name on it. Sarah, you wouldn't happen to know what bank Jonathan uses, would you?"

"I remember he used a few banks. I thought it odd at the time, but he said he didn't trust one financial institution with all his money. Let's see, he used Bank of New Jersey, Newhall Private, and there was a third one—a small one—oh, oh, Passaic Valley Bank."

"I think I'll give Zimmerman a call. Maybe he has some idea of how we can get more information about Jonathan's stash."

***

"Rita, I told you not to call me at work anymore. I have my uncle breathing down my neck and…"

"Look, you little idiot, we need to talk."

"About what?"

"Roy Thomas called me into his office for a little chat yesterday."

"What did the old fuddy-duddy have to say?"

"He intimated that if you and I were doing anything under-handed, say like embezzling money or something like that, we might unintentionally hurt other people who we cared about."

"Okay. But I don't see how this affects me, Rita."

Rita could feel her blood boiling. "You ungrateful little imbecile! He knows about the account you put under my son's name. I'm sure sweet little Sarah told him about it. He didn't say it in so many words, but he implied my Daniel could become involved in any proceedings that might take place. And you know that Daniel is already on probation for taking some money from his old boss. This could be the thing that puts him behind bars!"

"I suggest you calm down, Rita. First of all, I don't care what happens to Daniel. He's your son, not mine. Second, I purposely put his name on one of the accounts as an insurance policy that you would remain my ally. I guess it worked, huh? Third, you need to get yourself together. We've almost pulled this off, and I'm not going to let my uncle, Roy Thomas, Sarah, or you blow this for me. Now have a cup of tea, relax, and I'll stop by later so we can hash this out. Goodbye."

Rita couldn't believe her ears. When did she lose control of the situation? When did Jonathan get the upper hand in their relationship, and how the heck was she going to fix this? A cup of tea might just be the short-term answer after all.

***

Darn, darn, darn. The tea wasn't working. Rita's nerves were raw. Suddenly, she felt like she was alone without any allies. Mr. Thomas had threatened her with dismissal for violating his ethics contract, though Rita wasn't certain he could do that. Sarah couldn't even look her in the eye. Rita had never really considered Sarah a friend, but it was nice to be able to vent to her at times. And Jonathan…he could be a jerk, but she never felt like he had abandoned her before, until now. Jonathan threatened her son! How dare he. Daniel may be a problem child, but he was her problem child, and she wasn't going to let Jonathan touch a hair on his head.

She needed a plan. The first thing she needed to do was contact the banks. She knew of the three accounts that she and Jonathan had originally set up and at which banks they resided. She was listed on those accounts. Jonathan mentioned a fourth account, the one with Daniel's name on it. *He wouldn't be stupid enough to use one of the same banks, would he? She'd have to check. Knowing Jonathan, she was sure there was a fifth and possibly a sixth account that she wasn't aware of. How was she going to get her hands on those records?*

Okay, Rita think, think, think. If you were Jonathan, what would you do? That's it! Why didn't she think of this before? He'd call someone to do the dirty work for him. She'd call Harley Jacobsen. He was a former police officer turned private detective. Rita had dated Harley several years back, and he was still sweet on her. He even made Jonathan a little jealous. Harley was sophisticated and debonaire and a gentleman to boot…everything Jonathan wasn't. In fact, the last time she saw him, he had asked her what she saw in "that dumb kid." Rita was certain that Harley would help her. She just had to be careful how she presented the situation. If he thought she was involved in any hanky-panky, he may not want to get involved. Harley was an aboveboard kind of guy. Her biggest concern was the account with Daniel's name on it. If he could find out about any other accounts, that would be icing on the cake, but Rita needed to be sure that Daniel's future was safe. *Eureka!* She'd tell Harley that someone was trying to blackmail Daniel—it wasn't entirely a lie. *Here goes nothing.*

Harley was about to leave his office when the phone rang. "Hello, you have reached Harley Jacobsen Investigations. Harley here."

"Harley, hi this is Rita. Rita Polansky. I've been thinking about you and was wondering…"

"Rita, sweetheart, how are you? What can I do for you on this beautiful day?"

"My son has gotten himself into something of a jam, and I could use your professional help."

"Well, tell me, tell me."

"He's being blackmailed and I…"

Harley could hear the distress in Rita's voice. "Who is blackmailing him? Now, I can hear you're upset, so just take your time and tell me what's going on."

"You know that Daniel is often his own worst enemy. He's told me that he's being blackmailed. That someone set up a bank account in his name, and he's afraid that person is going to use it for nefarious purposes. And you know that Daniel is on parole…"

"Shhh. It's okay, Rita. I'm gonna help you. Did Daniel happen to mention who this person is and why someone would want to do that to him?"

"No, that's just it, Harley. He won't share that information with me. I just know that he's scared, and I'm scared for him. Is there anything we can do?"

"Why don't you have dinner with me tonight so we can discuss further, that is if you're not too busy with the youngster. What's his name again?"

"Harley Jacobsen! You know his name, and I've told you Jonathan is quite mature for his age."

"You always did have a great sense of irony, Rita. I'll pick you up at your place at 7:30 this evening."

"Thank you, Harley. I feel so much better now."

Rita took a deep breath. Harley bought her story hook, line, and sinker. Now she only had to figure out what she was going to wear to dinner.

A Date with Harley

Harley was right on time, dressed in a black suit, white shirt, and black-and-blue striped tie, topped off by his Stetson hat and cowboy boots. *He looked incredible.*

"You look stunning," Harley said as he lifted her up by her waist and swung her around. His hands remained on her waist even after he put her down. Rita had worn a blue dress that night that coincidentally matched Harley's tie.

"Let me grab a wrap," Rita said, as she ever so gently pushed his hands away from her waistline.

"Okay. All set," announced Rita, as she walked back into the room, with a light sweater, moments later.

Harley talked all the way to the restaurant. He was always a chatterbox, and normally, it didn't bother her, but tonight she was trying to focus on what she was going to tell him about the account, and he was disrupting her thoughts.

"Rita, darling, you're not laughing. I just told you one of my best jokes, one that always gets a laugh, and you're just sitting there. Have I lost my touch?"

Oh dear. At least try to be attentive, Rita scolded herself. "Sorry, Harley. I was lost in thought. You know, about Daniel."

"Oh, how cavalier of me. Of course, that's why you didn't laugh. I'll shut up for now, at least until we get to the restaurant."

Relieved not to hear his voice, at least for the interim, Rita continued to imagine how the conversation would go tonight and what Harley would want in payment for helping her. Before she knew it, Harley was handing his car keys to the valet, and her door was being held open. Rita had been to this restaurant, the Veranda Room, before. Not with Harley but with Jonathan.

"I hope you like this restaurant, Rita. I just learned about it, and it's quickly become one of my favorite haunts."

"Yes, actually, I believe I've been here before at least once or twice."

"Good evening, Ms. Polansky," said the maître d'.

"Once or twice? Harley arched his eyebrow. "Darlin', they know you by name. You've been here more than that. Care to share?"

"It's a woman's prerogative to keep some secrets, Mr. Jacobsen."

"Mr. Jacobsen? Huh."

Once they were seated, Rita hid behind the menu to avoid any other questions from Harley. After several minutes and a few deep cleansing breaths, she lowered her menu, smiling at Harley. "Well, I believe I know what I want," she said with a smile. "How about you?" Then she heard it—Jonathan's voice. He always had such poor timing. Or did he follow them to the restaurant? *Okay, calm down. You've been here before with Jonathan. Maybe it's just a coincidence that he's having dinner here tonight.*

"Rita…Harley. I didn't know you two were an item again. You old son of a gun," he said, lightly punching Harley in his bicep. "So, what are you two crazy kids up to tonight?" he asked, looking quizzically at Rita.

"That, my young man, is private," Harley answered. "Isn't it a school night?"

Rita watched as Jonathan's face flushed red and his hands clenched into fists at his sides. She was expecting steam to come out of the top of his head. But instead, Jonathan did the unexpected. He let out a rip-roaring laugh.

"A school night. That's a good one, buddy," he said, slapping Harley a little too hard on the back. "Tonight may be a school night, indeed, but I'm no longer in school. I may be young, but as Rita will attest, I'm just as good as any man out there, where it counts. See you around, Harley. Honey, why don't you give me a call later?" he said, winking at Rita.

"Well, that went well," Rita said, hoping to break the tension.

"Rita, I don't know what you and that hooligan have going on, and for once, I'm going to mind my own business. I'm here to try and help you solve Daniel's dilemma. I'm just not going to pursue anything in a romantic way until you tell me otherwise."

"Oh, Harley. I appreciate that. Let's order, and then we can talk about Daniel."

Harley was quiet during dinner. Rita was certain any romantic plans he had were dashed by Jonathan's earlier performance.

"A penny for your thoughts?" Rita asked Harley.

"Sorry. I'm just savoring my meal. So, let's try to figure out how we can save young Daniel from any further legal challenges."

Harley listened intently as Rita laid out just what she wanted him to know. She suggested some banks in town he might look into, and some of Daniel's friends he might want to talk to.

"Let me see what I come up with," said Harley. "I'll let you know how it's going over the next few days."

***

It had been a week and still no word from Harley. Rita couldn't help but wonder if he was trying to back out of his promise to help her. Her conversation with Jonathan that night after dinner was also weighing on her. That little idiot knew something was up, and he would sniff around until he found it. If he thought she was trying to double-cross him, he'd go right after Daniel. To quell Jonathan's jealousy, Rita assured him that she and Harley were out that evening as good friends and nothing more.

In the meantime, Harley realized his emotions for Rita were getting in the way. He decided to call in a favor from his friend and colleague, Tim Lawrence.

"How ya doing, buddy? Yeah, it's me, Harley. I'm doing great! Look I'd like you to do me one and check out someone named Daniel Polansky. Yeah.

That's it. P-o-l-a-n-s-k-y. His mom, Rita, is a friend, and she's convinced he's being blackmailed. I'd like to help her clear this up. I told her I'd look into it, but I may be a little too close to the situation, know what I mean? This kid's on the police radar already, and one more slip-up, and he's off to jail. I thought you could tap into some of your local police connections and dig up some stuff. Naw, Rita doesn't know who is trying to blackmail him. I'm sending everything I have to you via courier service this afternoon. Find out what you can. Okay, thanks, pal. I owe you one." *If Tim Lawrence can't turn something up on that kid, then I don't know who can.*

As he was dialing Rita's phone number, Harley couldn't stop thinking about how he and Rita would make a great couple and decided he'd put some thought into how to get the annoying school-boy out of the way. In fact, he's put a call into her right now, so she'd know she was on his mind and that he was working on her case.

"Hey, sweetheart! How are you on this fine day?"

"I'm great, Harley. I was just thinking about you. Have you thought of any ways to find out more about the bank account with Danny's name on them?"

"That's why I called. I spoke to my good friend, Tim Lawrence. He helps me out with my cases now and then. If Tim can't find out who's doing this to your boy, no one can."

Harley thought Rita would be pleased about this development, but instead, there was dead silence.

After a few moments, Harley said, "I have to say, your response isn't what I had anticipated. I thought it would be somewhere between "Yahoo!" and "That's great"—but silence isn't at all what I expected darlin'."

"Oh, it's just that I thought you would be the one handling this personally. I didn't want to involve too many people, you know, out of respect for Danny's privacy. How do I know Tim will be discreet?"

"As I said before Rita, Tim is one of the best investigators I know. He works with me a lot. He's a professional. He'd never share any information. Promise."

"I understand. I just don't know him, and so I don't trust him as much as I trust you, Harley. I don't want the people who set up this account coming after Danny or me."

"Don't you worry, darlin'. Tim is as closemouthed as they come. The only person he'll be talking to about this is me."

"Okay, Harley. I trust you."

"Gotta go, sweetheart. I'll talk to you later and let you know what develops."

Getting off the phone, Harley got the all too familiar feeling deep down in his gut when someone was lying to him. *Why was Rita lying?* What didn't she want him to know?

Rita didn't feel any better about the conversation. *What the heck! Why did Harley have to involve someone else? What if this guy came up with something that connected her to the account? On the other hand, if he somehow found out Jonathan was involved, that might give her the upper hand again.*

Rita was hoping that luck was with her on this one. But just to make sure, she'd take out her own little insurance policy.

CHAPTER 41

His Name Keeps Coming Up

"Sarah, I was talking to Mel Lerman. I think you've met him once or twice. He's an old friend from college. Anyway, I told him what was going on over at Zimmerman's, and he suggested I contact Tim Lawrence, who has helped him in the past with some private investigation work. He thought he might be able to provide us with some leads about the missing money. Since you've been doing the yeoman's share of the work on this case, I'd like you to fill Tim in on the details. I'll contact him, first, to lay the groundwork and ask him to follow up with you. You look concerned. Are you okay?"

"Oh, yes, Mr. Thomas. It's just that I don't want Jonathan to find out I've been talking to an investigator about him or Rita. I've been on the other end of his temper before, and it's not a pleasant place to be."

"You listen to me, young lady. Don't worry about Jonathan. He as much as touches you and that'll be the end of Mr. Silver." Noticing Sarah's grin, he added, "See, I got you to smile."

Sarah couldn't help it. Whenever Mr. Thomas assumed a fatherly role, it gave her a feeling of warmth and safety, something she only ever felt from Nate, Bubbe, and Mitzi.

"Let me know when Mr. Lawrence is going to call so that I can be prepared."

"Sure thing. Sarah, I may not tell you this often enough but thank you for being a part of my company. I consider you family. Now, don't cry," he said, watching as tears welled up in Sarah's eyes.

"I can't help it, Mr. Thomas. Sometimes you say the sweetest things," she said, dabbing her eyes with her handkerchief.

***

"May I speak to Tim Lawrence?"

"At your service. Who's callin'?"

"My name's Roy Thomas. I'm an accountant, and I've run into a little bit of a problem with one of my client's accounts."

"Someone skimmin' off the top?"

"Mel said you were good."

"Mel? The only Mel I know is Mel Lerman."

"That's him. He and I go way back."

"Geez, I haven't heard that name in a while. How the heck is he?"

"He's doing well. I was telling him about my problem, and he said you do great investigative work."

"Yep, I do."

"I'd like you to speak with my assistant, Sarah Steinman. She's the one who stumbled across the discrepancy and has been helping me uncover some information."

"You got it. Can I get a hold of her on the same number?"

"Yes, same one."

"Great. I'll give her a call now."

"Can you wait about half an hour before you call her? I want to give her a heads-up."

"Sure thing."

Hanging up the phone, Roy felt a bit more confident that this embezzlement was going to be wrapped up sooner than later.

Sarah was walking back to her desk from the powder room when she heard the loud bbrrnngg, bbrrnngg from her desk phone.

"Yes, Mr. Thomas?"

"Sarah, you okay? You sound out of breath."

"I'm good."

"If you say so. Tim Lawrence should be contacting you shortly. Feel free to answer his questions and provide him with any information he may need. We need to find out just how Rita and Jonathan have set up this scheme."

Just as she started entering figures into the general ledger, Sarah's phone rang again.

"Hello, Thomas Finance Company, how may I assist you today?"

"I was told this was the number for Sarah Steinman. Can you tell her Tim Lawrence is callin'?"

"Hi, Mr. Lawrence. This is Sarah. Mr. Thomas said you would be calling."

"I'd like to get some details on the Zimmerman case. Can I stop by the office tomorrow, say between 10:00 a.m. and 11:00 a.m.?"

"Of course, I'll see you then, Mr. Lawrence."

Sarah could feel her stomach acting up again. Every time she felt anxious about something, she felt it in her gut first.

The next morning, at precisely 10:00 a.m., Tim Lawrence was at the front door of Thomas Finance Co. peering through the window. He saw a young woman sitting at a desk with her back to the door. Not wanting to startle her, Tim first knocked on the glass and then entered the office.

"Miss Steinman?"

"Oh, you must be Mr. Lawrence," she said as she turned around. He was so handsome but in a non-Jewish sort of way.

Tim couldn't believe his luck. Not only did he get a new gig, but he got to spend time with such a looker.

"Call me...Tim." *Almost forgot my name there for a second. What the heck is going on? I never do that.* "Okay, let's get the ball rollin'. Can we talk in the conference room?"

"Follow me, Mr. Lawrence, I mean, Tim, and you can call me Sarah."

Tim's eyes roamed around the room, catching glimpses of the conference room table, the plaques, and the bookcases that lined the walls. He wanted to look anywhere but at Sarah, who for some reason, made him sweat.

"Why don't you walk me through how you found the error and what's happened since then."

"That's a tall order. Okay, let's see. Mr. Thomas asked me to do some work on a client's account—Zimmerman Company. It was a big deal because…"

Tim took notes as Sarah took him through the months-long saga of the missing funds.

"…and then I asked Rita to help me go over the numbers since she initially was working on the account and…"

"Okay, stop there. Who is Rita?"

"Rita works here—or at least she did—it's complicated."

"For now, just give me a last name for Rita."

"Polansky. That's P-o—"

"Polansky?" Tim interrupted. "Rita Polansky?"

"Yes, that's right. Why?"

Could it be the same Rita Polansky that Harley mentioned? It wouldn't be the first time two of his cases collided.

"Oh, no reason. It's just not a common name, that's all. A friend mentioned someone by that name, but I'm sure it's not the same person. I think that's enough for today. Can we talk again tomorrow?"

"Mr. Thomas told me to make myself available to you, so just tell me what time you want to stop by."

"Let's discuss it over lunch." Tim would be sure to choose a place with a bar where he could get a drink to calm his nerves. *What was it about this girl?*

CHAPTER 42

Getting to Know Sarah

Tim made some phone calls and headed over to Thomas Finance Co. to pick up Sarah for lunch. She had filled him in on the basics, but there were still some aspects of the case that were gnawing at him. Sarah was on the telephone when Tim arrived. He quietly sat down at Rita's desk so he was out of her direct view. When the call ended, she began closing up the ledgers on her desk, humming to herself. Sarah was happy that Tim was on his way over. She enjoyed his company, even though she knew her relationship with him would likely only remain professional. He sure was handsome, but she was equally certain that he wasn't Jewish. As Sarah stood and turned around, she shrieked.

Clutching her chest with both hands, she blurted out, "Oh good Lord. Tim, you scared me. Don't do that ever again."

Hearing the commotion, Mr. Thomas poked his head out of his partially opened office door.

"Are you okay, Sarah?" he asked. "I'm fine, Mr. Thomas."

As Sarah and Tim walked toward the front door, Mr. Thomas wondered if Sarah was as smitten with Tim as he seemed to be with her. "You take care of our Sarah now, you hear me, Mr. Lawrence?"

What does he think I'm planning to do to her? Why is he so over-protective of Sarah? He is her boss, not her father, Tim thought. After promising Mr. Thomas that he would handle Sarah with kid gloves, Tim whispered to Sarah, "I didn't expect that reaction at all from you. Are you always so skittish?"

"I just didn't hear you arrive, and then I turned around and you were there. I don't like people sneaking up on me. I don't like surprises at all. They don't seem to work out in my favor. Let's get going. Where would you like to eat?"

"I noticed a little place at the corner. Turnbull's Bar."

"I don't think it's appropriate for me to go into a bar. Besides, I can't eat anything they sell in there. And I'm sure my grandmother would have something to say about me being seen in a bar with a man. Let's try Benny's. I can get a salad there. Come on, we need to hurry before it gets too crowded."

After opening the door to the deli, Tim realized what Sarah was talking about. The room itself was small, maybe fifteen by twenty feet, stuffed with wooden chairs and tables almost on top of one another. Pictures of the owner sporting a white apron, surrounded by family, hung on the wall.

"Are we going to be able to talk here?" asked Tim, looking around at what seemed like utter chaos. "It's kinda noisy."

"Oh, you'll get used it," Sarah said, raising her voice. "The food's good, so a lot of businesspeople in the neighborhood stop here for lunch. They're so busy with their own conversations they won't hear us." Sarah was amused by Tim's hesitancy. Another sign that he didn't grow up in a Jewish home where loud voices and crowded rooms were not uncommon.

"Okay, if you say so, Sarah."

Sarah spotted Hazel, her favorite waitress at Benny's, and waved her over to their table. Hazel was a character. Born and bred in Passaic, she wore her hair teased in a bouffant style with a pencil behind one ear and a cigarette behind the other. Sometimes she would use the pencil as a barrette of sorts to hold back her bangs. Today was one of those days.

"Hi, hon. How are you?" Hazel asked, while removing her pencil, which had become intertwined in her hair.

Leaning in closer to the waitress, Sarah said, "I'm good, Hazel. I'd like you to meet my friend, Tim."

"Oh, your friend? What happened to the other friend you brought in here a couple of times?"

"Oh, oh…No, not that kind of friend. Tim and I are business associates. He's helping one of our clients."

"Okay, hon. You tell yourself whatever gets you through the day. What can I get you today? Let me guess, a green salad, no dressing, two hard-boiled eggs, and a hot tea."

"You always remember my order. Yes, that's exactly what I want."

"And for you, sir?" Hazel asked Tim.

"You got any alcohol here?"

"No alcoholic drinks here. But we've got food, you hungry?"

"Yeah, let me see. I'll have roast beef on white toast with mayo and ketchup. And do you have any cheese you can throw on there?" Hazel and Sarah exchanged glances. "What?" asked Tim.

"He's not from around here, is he, hon?" Turning to address Tim, Hazel answered, "I can't put cheese on it. I can give you a Kaiser roll or rye bread, but not white."

Leaning forward, Tim inquired, "What about the ketchup and mayo?"

"Sure, I can give you that on the side if you like." Sighing deeply and walking back to the kitchen, Sarah could hear Hazel say to no one in particular, "Live and learn."

Watching her walk away, Tim commented, "She's interesting, in an odd sort of way."

"I think she was making reference to your asking for white bread with meat and cheese and ketchup and mayo. That's quite an uncommon order for a kosher deli. The normal order would be roast beef on rye with mustard. And definitely no cheese."

"Well, I'm not like other people, Sarah," Tim noted, shrugging his shoulders. He didn't think his order was out of the ordinary; then again, he had never been to a Jewish deli before. Never to let a life lesson get the better of him, Tim made a mental note of how to order deli-style.

"So, let's talk about these missing funds, but before we do, I'm curious, who's the guy the waitress was talking about?" Watching as Sarah's face took on varying shades of red, Tim quickly added, "But tell me if it's none of my business."

"He's an ex-boyfriend. It's complicated. You may have seen his name in the file—Jonathan Silver."

"Yeah, he's the nephew of your client, Leonard Zimmerman, right?"

"Yes, that's how I met him. I thought he really liked me, but it turned out I was just a ruse to cover up his embezzlement plan."

"You sure he's involved?"

"Yes. I'm positive about that. Even Mr. Thomas thinks he is. We just can't prove it, which is why you were recommended. And if I'm right, he's also getting help from someone else."

"You got a name?" Tim inquired.

"Yes. Rita Polansky."

There's that name again. Who is this Rita Polansky? he wondered. "If you remember, I mentioned her name to you yesterday, when we spoke on the phone. She works at Thomas Finance with me. She used to be a friend until I found out what she was really like."

"She still working there?"

"I don't even know anymore, it's…"

"I know. It's complicated," Tim said with a huge grin on his face.

"Don't make fun of me." Sarah was doing her best to hide her nervousness, and now here he was, teasing her.

"I'm not making fun of you. I would never dream of doing that. It just seems to be one of your favorite phrases. It's my job to pick up on things like that. Besides, most things I encounter in my line of work are complicated. Complicated things keep me in business!"

Surprisingly, the food came in short order, despite the fact that the restaurant was so crowded. After taking the first bite of his sandwich, Tim moaned with satisfaction.

"I'm in heaven."

Sarah and Tim talked about the Zimmerman case between bites.

Before she realized it, her lunch hour was coming to an end.

"Look at the time," said Sarah, jumping to her feet. "I have to get back to work."

"Yeah, me too. Look, I still have some questions for you. Maybe we can do this again next week?"

"Sure. I'd like that." *Oops, did I just say that out loud?*

Tim was handsome in a rugged sort of way, but he was dangerous territory. Not like Jonathan or Henry dangerous; she was pretty sure he would never verbally or physically abuse her. No, Tim was the type of guy she could see herself falling for, and she was sure he wasn't Jewish, especially after his lunch order. Whatever this was between them could not grow beyond a working relationship. It just couldn't, as much as she wished it could. Walking Sarah back to Thomas Finance, Tim realized how much he liked her. But pursing those feelings would be breaking his number one rule: No mixing business with pleasure.

CHAPTER 43

A Bank Connection

S o far, no luck. Tim had been on the phone all morning, trying to get a handle on this bank account in Daniel Polansky's name. Luckily for him, he never threw away a number. Early in his career as a private investigator, he learned to keep every piece of paper he wrote something down on because you never know when you're going to need it. And Tim needed the help, of an acquaintance, Jack Gates, who was a VP at one of the banks Harley had mentioned. Maybe he'd cooperate. It never hurts to ask, something else Tim had learned in his line of work.

"Hi, this is Tim Lawrence. We met at a Christmas party in Doug Wartham's office last year. I'm doing fine. Yep. That was one helluva party. How are you?

Great. Listen, I'm in a predicament, and I need some advice. I'm working on a case for a friend. He knows a woman whose son is being blackmailed. He's been told there's a bank account in his name, and if he doesn't do what they want, they'll frame him for a crime. The kid's already knee-deep in doo-doo.

Yeah. I'm usually good at finding things that can't be found, but this time, I'm stuck. No bank is going to give me access to a depositor's account.

No. I haven't gone that route yet. Getting a court order is such a hassle. I'll have to talk to my friend and see how he wants to proceed. Uh-huh. Yeah, that's an idea. I'd appreciate that. Thanks."

Jack had told Tim he had four choices:

1. Put a tail on Mr. Silver to see if he can lead you to the bank or banks in question.
2. Go to the local banks, speak with the bank managers, explain the situation, and see if they are willing to release information, such as who was the signatory for the account under the name Daniel Polansky.
3. If that did not work, and he didn't have high hopes that it would, his next suggestion was to go to a judge for a court order.
4. And then, pray a lot, and hope something gives.

Tim hadn't been to church in years. He wasn't even sure God was listening anymore. Mulling over the choices, Tim realized he had an even bigger problem. He wasn't sure he could help Harley out if his friend was to be implicated in a fraudulent situation. He needed to speak with Harley right away.

But before he did that, he needed to review the information he had gathered thus far. He began writing a facts checklist, something he had always used to keep himself on track.

1. A Rita Polansky was a close friend of Harley's.
2. Rita's son, Daniel, was supposedly being blackmailed by individuals who threatened to frame him for a crime. They told him they opened a bank account in his name. So far there is no proof the account exists.
3. Rita had worked for and possibly is still working for Thomas Finance Co.
4. Sarah and Rita had been friends until something happened. What was that something?
5. Rita may be involved in the embezzlement at Zimmerman Co., but Jonathan Silver is still the prime suspect.

6.   Rita had (or has) some type of relationship with Jonathan
     Silver. What is it exactly?

Tim reached for his top right desk drawer where he kept his
trustworthy bottle of Bayer aspirin. This case was giving him a mean
headache. Before he even had a chance to pop it in his mouth, his
phone rang. "Lawrence, here. Hey, Harley. Yeah, man, I was just
thinking about you. Yeah, I've been doing some sniffing around.
Listen, can I ask you about your friend, Rita?"

"Well, that depends on your questions," Harley said with a
hearty laugh.

"Yeah, nothing like that Harley. First off, does your friend Rita
Polansky work for Thomas Finance Company?"

"Sure does. She's one of the best little bookkeepers this side of
the Mississippi."

"Look, Harley, I'm not sure I can help you with this case."

"Why is that?" asked Harley.

"Because I've just been hired by the guy who owns Thomas
Finance Company to help him figure out a client's embezzlement
case and Rita's name has come up as possibly being complicit in the
fraud."

So that's what Rita was hiding from him. *What else was she lying
about?* Harley was fit to be tied.

"Harley," asked Tim, "is there any chance I can speak directly
with Daniel or his mother?"

"I'll speak with Rita, but she told me she doesn't want to get
Daniel involved in this mess. Hey, Tim, I understand that you can't
officially help me, but would you mind keeping me up to date on
Rita's involvement? I know, I'm asking a lot, but she means a great
deal to me, and I just don't want to see her get hurt."

"I'll do what I can without compromising my client, Harley,
but no promises."

Moments after getting off the phone with Harley, it rang again.
It was Jack, his bank contact. "I didn't expect to hear back from you
so soon. Yeah. Hang on, I want to write this down."

Opening his desk drawer he saw pencils galore, a few erasers, but no pens. Why were there never any pens to be found when he needed them? As a last-ditch effort, he looked in his jacket pocket and found a pen. Before getting back on the call, he tested it out on the back of an envelope to make sure it wasn't out of ink.

"Okay, Jack, shoot. Are you sure? Uh-huh. Thanks."

Jack told Tim he had spoken with a friend at another bank. After a little cajoling and promising to wine and dine him, his friend divulged that he might be able to offer some help.

Tim wrote down the account number and name of the person who opened it. "I'll be damned."

CHAPTER 44

Life Gets Complicated

Nate had been watching Sarah pace from the kitchen to the living room for a good half hour. He knew something was wrong, but she seemed so agitated he wasn't sure how to approach her. On the other hand, he didn't want to leave her alone either.

"Sarah, I'm going to take a walk to the grocery store. Want to join me?"

"The store?"

"Yeah, the store. You know, the building on Main Street that has different kinds of food. I have this bad habit. I get hungry three times a day, and we've run out of some things. I promised Bubbe I would stop at the store sometime today. Before I get any dizzier watching you pace back and forth, I thought now might be a good time to go."

"Sure. I'll take a walk with you."

Now was his chance to find out why his sister was so stressed and anxious lately. "So, what's new? I haven't had a chance to sit down and speak with you recently. What's going on? Did I do anything to upset you?"

"Oh no, Nate. You didn't do anything." Sarah wanted to tell Nate what was going on, but she had promised Mr. Thomas that she wouldn't talk about the investigation. He didn't want Rita or Jonathan to get tipped off. And then there was Tim. She enjoyed spending time with him more than almost anyone else, but he wasn't Jewish, and her family, including Nate, would never approve. She had known him for such a short time, but she was more comfortable with him than she had ever been with Jonathan. She trusted him, instinctively.

"What gives, Sarah? Why the long face? What's going on, sis?"

"My life used to be so simple—you know. You, David, Steven, Bubbe, our aunts and uncles, Mitzi. Now it's anything but simple. It's changing every day—new situations, new people, new problems."

"No judgment here. You talk, and I'll listen. That's the way our conversations usually work, don't they?"

"Nate, are you accusing me of taking over a conversation?" Sarah asked, feigning haughtiness, hands placed on her hips.

"Well, not today, but usually that's the way it goes, sis."

"You can always make me laugh, Nate."

"Okay, so the long face is gone. Now we just have to work on why you're so sad. Seriously, Sarah, what is going on? I'm worried. Bubbe's worried. I think even Steven and David are starting to pick up on your odd mood."

Bubbe's worried? That's the last thing Sarah wanted. Since Bubbe's heart attack, Sarah had been extra careful not to upset her grandmother.

"Things at work have been crazy, Nate. Mr. Thomas has me working on finding out who stole from Mr. Zimmerman, our client, and I'm just mentally and physically exhausted from it. I just can't talk about it. That's all."

Nate could see Sarah was tired and maybe even a little scared. "Sarah, I would never ask you to betray a trust. But I have a feeling there's something besides the investigation going on, something that's making you question yourself. What is it?"

She took a deep breath in and let it out slowly. This was not going to be an easy conversation.

"I met this guy, Nate. He's helping with the investigation. Mr. Thomas told me I should give him as much of my time as he required—and I have. Whenever I do, I don't want the conversation to end. I know that sounds crazy…"

"It doesn't sound crazy, Sarah. It sounds like you like this guy. That's good. Now you can finally get over that schmo, Jonathan. So, what's this guy's name?"

"Tim Lawrence."

"Huh." *Tim isn't usually a Jewish first name although Lawrence could go either way,* he thought. "Not related to the singer Steve Lawrence, is he, Sarah? Cause that would be the cat's meow."

"Nate! This isn't funny. I can't sleep. I can't eat. All I do is think about him. I don't think he's Jewish. I mean I haven't asked—it hasn't come up—I just don't think he is. That's my dilemma. Nothing romantic has happened yet, but being around him makes me happy. Okay, I said it. But you have to promise me that you won't say a word to Bubbe or anyone else. I don't want to be the cause of Bubbe's next heart attack. Please, Nate. This has to be our secret."

"Okay, okay, I get it. I won't tell Bubbe, but you have to promise me that you'll think about ending this before it becomes a big deal. I mean it. You are just too different. You don't fit into his world, and he doesn't fit into yours. It's never going to work."

Nate hated seeing his sister so upset. He knew this kind of stress would lead to mental, emotional, even physical issues, none of which would he wish on anyone. He himself suffered from chronic migraines and stomach issues. You'd think after millennia of dealing with angst, Jews would be better with handling anxiety. Personally, he didn't care if Sarah married a Jewish guy or not, he just wanted her to be happy, but Bubbe and his aunts and uncles were going to have a different perspective on this. They had always been clear on that one point—dating outside of the Jewish community was verboten. Nate could see their point. Being Jewish wasn't just their faith; it was their culture, their food, their language, their very being. He'd have to figure out a way to help Sarah get through this.

CHAPTER 45

Rita Is Playing Games

Tim had been trying to get a hold of Harley all morning. He had some new information for him, but Harley wasn't picking up the telephone. Maybe he had gone out to meet with a client. Tim wondered if the account with Daniel Polansky's name on it was somehow connected with the Zimmerman embezzlement. It was beginning to seem like much more than a possibility.

The account in Daniel Polansky's name had two other names on it as cosigners. One was Rita Polansky and the other, Jonathan Silver. He hoped Harley might be able to shed some light on why his friend Rita would send him on a wild goose chase. *She was a cosigner on the damn account. Why was she acting like she didn't know?* Something fishy was going on, and Tim was going to get to the bottom of it.

Just as his stomach began rumbling, reminding him to eat lunch, he got a call from Harley.

"Hey, Tim. Harley here. Any news?"

"Funny you should ask. I tried calling you several times this morning."

"You caught me red-handed. I was practicing my golf swing at the driving range. Nothing like hitting a bucket of balls in the morning."

"Glad you were out enjoying yourself while the rest of us were working. I think I have some news for you, though I'm not sure you're gonna like it."

"Why's that?"

"Well, it seems like your friend Rita is playing games with you. My contact told me that the individuals who opened the account with Daniel Polansky's name, at the Bank of New Jersey, were a Rita Polansky and Jonathan Silver. Unless there's someone else with your friend's same name, this lady is lying to you."

"Aw, hell. Rita told me she was done with that little twerp. She seemed so sincere about not knowing about the account. Could Silver have started it without her knowing about it?" he asked.

"Sure. He would have had to forge her name on the signature card." Tim had been doing this job for over a decade, and he knew that anything was possible, but his instincts told him that Rita wasn't an innocent bystander; she was involved.

Harley was silent on the other end of the phone. "I think Rita's gotten herself into quite a pickle this time. And I'm not too sure I'm going to be able to help her out of it. Okay, thanks for the info, Tim."

"Okay, Harley, this will be the last thing I can tell you because I'm working on the other end of this case. Take care of yourself."

After hanging up with Harley, Tim was reminded once more of lunch, not by his hunger pangs this time, but by a call from Thomas Finance Co.

"Tim, hi, it's Sarah. I was wondering if you could stop by today to talk about the case. I'm free for lunch if you are."

Sarah's call brought a smile to his face. He couldn't resist teasing her. "Are you asking me out for lunch, Ms. Steinman?"

"Uh—no—yes—I guess I am. Look, I'm not usually this forward, but you seem like a nice guy, and I'd like to get to know you better. There—I said it."

"Well, how can I refuse an offer like that? What if I pick up some sandwiches, and we have them in your conference room? It'll be quieter than the last place we talked."

"Sounds great, but I'll take a green salad, no dressing, if you don't mind."

"Anything for a client."

Hanging up the phone, Tim had a feeling that Sarah was becoming much more than a client, and he wasn't sure that was such a good idea.

He found her sitting in the conference room when he arrived at Thomas Finance. Placing the lunch bags on the table, he announced, "Your delivery is here. You know it's customary to give the delivery man a tip," he said, sticking out his hand.

Laughing at his comment, Sarah asked, "What are you implying? Here's a tip. Always treat a lady with respect."

"Ouch, okay I deserve that. Where's Mr. Thomas?" Tim asked. "I wanted to talk to him a bit more."

"He's gone out for a business lunch, but he should be back before we're done. Now, kindly hand me my salad, sir."

As he passed the salad with no dressing to her, wondering how someone so exceptional could eat something so bland, he said, "Sarah, you mentioned early on that you had your suspicions about Rita and Jonathan. Why do you think that?"

"Well, as I told you before, Jonathan was obviously upset with me when I originally reported the missing funds to Mr. Thomas. He even proposed marriage to me to get me to stop looking into it. He wanted me as his wife so he could control what I saw or said.

"When I asked Rita to help review the books with me because she was the one who took care of the Zimmerman account before I did, she came back and told me she didn't find any problems. When I told her that wasn't possible because I went over those books with a fine-tooth comb, she laughed and made some joke about young people thinking they know everything. I don't think I know everything, but I'm good at keeping books, and I know I didn't…"

"Whoa. Is that why you and Rita aren't friends any longer?"

"Not exactly. I found out that she and Jonathan have been having an affair, even while he was dating me. I felt like such a fool."

"Bingo!"

"That's an odd response."

"Not if you knew what I know," Tim said as he got up from his seat. "I've gotta go now. Tell Mr. Thomas I'll give him a call. I think I may be on to something here."

"Wait a minute. Onto what?"

"I need to do a little more digging before I share that."

"O-kay. Good luck."

"Luck is what you make of it, Sarah." Tim winked and then walked out the front door.

Watching him leave, she wished her circumstances were different. He was such a nice guy.

***

After getting back to his office, Tim wondered if there were other bank accounts that might have the name of Rita Polansky or Jonathan Silver attached to them. He called Roy Thomas to find out Rita's address. Once he had that, he could begin to look more closely into Rita and her financial dealings. His investigative juices were flowing.

Harley had said he believed her to be struggling financially. As it turned out, though, she had several well-stocked bank accounts, though only a few in her name. Most were in names of companies he was now sure were fictitious. But her name was on them as the person to contact. *Amateur move.* Tim chuckled to himself.

He was one step closer to connecting Rita and Jonathan to the Zimmerman embezzlement. His next step was to call Roy Thomas and update him on the information he had uncovered. He wanted to tell Harley, but Roy was his client, and he needed to protect that relationship first and foremost.

"Hello, Mr. Thomas, It's Tim Lawrence. Yes, thank you for the address; it was extremely useful. I think you'll be happy with what I've found out. It seems your trusted senior bookkeeper has repeatedly been sticking her fingers into the honeypot. I found several accounts where she is the contact person. And the accounts totaled close to a hundred thousand dollars in them, including one in her son's name."

"That's great, my boy!" Mr. Thomas realized that now they had to connect Jonathan to those accounts. He was certain Rita was not doing this alone.

"I just need Jonathan's address," Tim said, breaking his concentration. "Can you get that for me?"

"In a flash," Mr. Thomas noted. "I'll call you back."

Within ten minutes, he was reading Jonathan's address off to Tim. "Tell me if you need anything else."

Tim had been making calls for two hours and nothing. Maybe Jonathan was smarter than he thought. Maybe he didn't put any of the accounts in his name but instead used family to cover up his tracks.

"Sorry to bother you twice in one day, Mr. Thomas. Can you tell me if Jonathan Silver has any siblings? No, huh. What are his parents' names? Okay. That's E-v-e-l-y-n. You said his father, Charles, is deceased?

All right. I believe that our Mr. Silver put money he took from his uncle and deposited it into accounts that have a trusted family member's name on them. Yeah, like his mother's. I'll let you know what I find out."

Nothing unusual about the accounts listed under Evelyn Silver.

Those turned out to be a dead end. Tim's mind kept going back to Sarah and what she had told him about Rita and Jonathan, that they had been having an affair. What if it was more than that? What if they were secretly married? It may be far-fetched, but he had to check it out.

After a full two days of calling the banks and his contacts at the Office of Vital Statistics, he had his answer. The bank had just sent him a document via courier.

"Yes! Bingo!" he exclaimed, looking at the piece of paper in front of him. There was a list of accounts—several with the name Rita Silver on them, some with company names on them, but the same contact information as for Rita Polansky. Jonathan may have proposed to Sarah, but he couldn't have legally married her. He was already married to Rita.

Tim called Mr. Thomas, who couldn't contain his excitement. "Hot damn, boy. You are good. Send me a report and anything else you turn up, and I'll forward it to Zimmerman."

CHAPTER 46

Bubbe's Reaction to Tim

"Mamala, vhat's vrong? You've had your kishkas in knots lately."

Sarah stopped herself from laughing. Her stomach was bothering her. Kishka's are intestines. It was unnerving how her grandmother could pinpoint her moods.

"I'm okay, Bubbe. We need to talk."

Molly didn't say a word to her granddaughter but wondered if Jonathan was back in the picture. And if he was, so help her…Well, she wasn't certain what she would do, but it would involve screaming, on her part.

"Bubbe, I told you that I've been working with Mr. Thomas and a private investigator on this embezzlement case, but what I haven't shared is that I really like the investigator. He's such a sweet guy. He's smart, and he's handsome, and he treats me so well. Just so you know, we're not dating, but we have had some lunches together."

"Mamala, I'm a bit confused. If he's such a good catch, then vhy haven't you brought him home yet?"

"Because you won't approve, Bubbe."

"Vhat's not to approve? He treats you vell, and he's handsome and smart. Vhat's vrong vith him?"

"Well, for starters his name is Tim Lawrence, and I'm fairly sure he's not Jewish." Sarah took a few steps back just in case the fireworks began.

Molly was at a loss for words. The good news was it wasn't that awful Jonathan Silver. The bad news was he wasn't of the Jewish faith, and Bubbe couldn't allow that to happen. Taking her grand-daughter's hands in hers, she said, "Mamala, I know that life often brings us temptations that ve vish ve could take because it vould make us happy in the moment. But believe me vhen I tell you that your perfect young man is not going to seem so perfect when he doesn't celebrate the same holidays as you or believe in HaShem. And vhat about the children…oy, are they going to be confused. Please, Sarah, think about it. I von't demand that you stop this relationship before it becomes any more involved because you are now a young woman and that has to be your decision. But I vill strongly suggest that you consider doing so…for the sake of our family's sake. I'm going to give you time to think about vhat I said. I'll be in my room if you need to talk."

What am I going to do now? Sarah knew that even though Bubbe invited her to further discuss the topic, the only thing she really wanted to hear from her granddaughter was that it was over. *Why was life so complicated?* And why was HaShem constantly throw-ing a wrench into her plans?

CHAPTER 47

A Friendly Chat

I n an effort to clean up some of the assorted piles on his desk, Tim decided to stop at his office on Sunday, which was unusual for him, but he needed to catch up on some paperwork. He was going through some case details when he got a phone call from a guy named Nate Steinman. Nate explained to Tim that he was Sarah's older brother.

He asked Tim if they could meet and talk man to man. When Tim inquired as to why he wanted to meet him, he said, "I want to get to know the guy my little sister is so hung up on." Nate invited Tim out for a beer at McNaulty's Pub later that day, and as the good Irish boy he was, he couldn't pass up a beer—could he?

The pair seemed to hit it off. Nate and Tim were about the same age. They both liked the New York Giants and hated the Philadelphia Eagles, but Tim was a big-time Boston Red Sox fan while Nate was an ardent New York Yankees fan.

Sarah's name finally came up, although Tim couldn't remember whether he or Nate had broached the subject. Tim confided in Nate that he was intrigued by Sarah. She was funny, intelligent, and had a wicked sense of humor. He realized they came from two completely different backgrounds, but Tim didn't see that as an obstacle. However, he would soon to discover that Nate definitely did.

Nate explained how Bubbe and their aunts and uncles were an important source of support for all the kids, especially Sarah, and that their opinions counted for a lot. One of their strongest opinions was that Sarah should date and marry someone Jewish. Tim didn't like where the conversation was headed, but he understood. Several years back, his cousin Eileen had dated an Irish guy, who was Protestant, and you would have thought by the reaction of his aunt and others that the world had come off its axis.

Before leaving the bar, Nate said, "Look, Tim. You seem to be a nice guy. You've got a good job, you dress decently, and if you were Jewish, I would bring you home to Bubbe myself—but you're not. I'd appreciate it if you didn't tell Sarah that we spoke. I told her I'd be supportive, and I'm doing my best here, but I have to worry about how the family will deal with this too. It's not just about Sarah. I'm asking you, if she pursues a romantic relationship, to kindly back off and let her down gently. That way, I get to keep my promise to Sarah and keep peace in the Steinman family."

Tim nodded, still not quite sure why he was allowing someone to tell him what to do with his life, but he could tell Nate cared about Sarah and so did he. In the end, it just seemed like the right thing to do.

Different Worlds

Several days had passed since Tim sent everything he had uncovered to Mr. Thomas. Although he hadn't heard directly from him, Tim had an idea of what was going on as he and Sarah had lunch a few times since then. Roy Thomas passed the information to Leonard Zimmerman who had spoken with the Passaic District Attorney. Rita and Jonathan were on their way to an embezzlement charge, and his opportunity to spend time with Sarah, outside of a real date, was dwindling. Truth be told, Tim knew the relationship was dead in the water but didn't want to have to hurt Sarah.

She was everything he had always wanted in a woman, but he knew he didn't fit into her world. He'd have to let her down easy. He didn't want to make her feel as if something was wrong with her—*It just wasn't going to work out.*

Tim called Sarah and suggested they meet after work at Thomas Finance.

Arriving at the office, he told Sarah about the charges against the Silvers. "Hey, Sarah. I just found out that the Passaic District Attorney has enough evidence against Jonathan and Rita to press charges."

"I don't like to revel in someone else's misery, but they so deserve it. They hurt so many people, Tim."

Robin L.R. Kellogg

"Yeah. Hurting people is never a good thing. Sarah, you were honest with me about your feelings, and I want to be honest with you. Okay?"

Uh-oh. Not sure I like the sound of that, she thought. "Sure, Tim, you can tell me anything."

"Sarah, you are beautiful and smart and one of the most honest people I know, but you know whatever this is between us isn't going to work, right? We're just too different. I don't fit into your world, and you don't fit into mine."

Huh. That was the same thing Nate had said to her when she told him about Tim. *Oh, was he going to get an earful!*

Sarah was determined to continue her friendship with Tim as long as she could. "I can try, I really can, Tim. Please."

"I don't want you to change for me. You're perfect the way you are. I hope there won't be any awkwardness between us." Tim wasn't sure how Sarah felt, but he hated himself for agreeing to end things with her.

"I see. You're not giving me a choice, are you? You should go, Tim. I need to be alone at the moment." All Sarah could think about was calling her brother Nate and finding out why he insisted on interfering in her love life.

"Hey, sis. What's wrong? I can hear you crying."

"Nathan Steinman, what did you say to him?"

"I'm not sure I know what you're talking about, sis."

"Oh, don't try to fool me. I knew it. I knew that I shouldn't have told you about my feelings for Tim because you did what you always do and interfere!"

Oh geez, he thought. "Honestly, I have no idea what you're talking about. I'll be right there to pick you up, kiddo. Let me tell Bubbe that I'm going out. Bye."

As Nate drove over to Thomas Finance to pick up his sister, he thought about how he was glad he had a chance to meet Tim and speak with him. Sarah may have an inkling about what happened, but he would never confirm it for her. After Sarah told Nate about her feelings for Tim, Nate had found his number in the local telephone directory and gave him a call. He wanted to know the guy his little sister was going gaga over. Tim turned out to be a good guy. When he found out the challenges Sarah would face with Bubbe and his aunts and uncles, because he wasn't Jewish, he did the gentlemanly thing and stepped aside. Nate respected him for that. It showed that Tim cared about Sarah. Nate promised Tim that Sarah would never know about their discussion. It would be their little secret. Nate never did admit that he spoke to Tim, but Sarah knew her brother, and realized that as annoying as it was, he interfered out of his concern and love for her.

***

Sarah was excited at how the case shaped up and was proud of her part in it. Things were all falling into place. Jonathan and Rita had their fingerprints on several accounts, thirteen in all. It turned out that there were not one but five accounts in Daniel's name. No big surprise there. Jonathan was protecting himself and making sure Rita stayed in line.

Six other accounts were in fictitious vendors and all named Jonathan and Rita as account signatories. The final two bank accounts were in the name of Mr. and Mrs. J. R. Silver. Tim was right. Jonathan and Rita had gotten married so that they wouldn't be able to testify against one another.

With this proof, Mr. Zimmerman could get the police and the FBI involved, as at least one of the banks was in New York City. Unfortunately, that meant that Rita's son, Daniel, might also be dragged into this, but that was one of many things that Sarah had learned she had no control over.

The DA ended up pressing embezzlement charges against Jonathan and Rita. Both pled not guilty, and there was a trial. It was the biggest scandal that happened in Passaic since the city treasurer ran away with tax-payer funds. The jury deliberated for two hours. That's all it took for them to convict Jonathan and Rita of the charges. Sarah, Mr. Zimmerman, and Mr. Thomas were all in the courtroom, that day, to see that justice was served. The judge gave Jonathan ten years in jail and Rita probation for three years and made her legally promise to never hold another job that dealt with finances. Her involvement couldn't be tied to the deposits, and besides, her testimony to prosecutors about the embezzlement plan and Jonathan's part in it was golden.

Sarah often reflected on her time with Tim and wished their circumstances had been different. In another life, maybe it would have worked out. He was such a sweet guy, though. Who did she know who would be perfect for him? *Mitzi!* She'd have to introduce him to Mitzi.

As for this life, Nate kept bringing up his Jewish pal, Marv Abelman, who he worked with, as a possible romantic match. *He could be such a nudge.*

"Okay. Okay. Set up a lunch and you can take me to meet him. But promise me if I go and sparks don't fly, you won't keep harping on this."

***

Much to Sarah's surprise the introduction to Marv went well, so well that they planned a date for the following week. She hoped that none of the nonsense she experienced with Jonathan would rear its ugly head. At least, Marv seemed sane. But she sure would feel more comfortable if Mitzi could come on the date with her. Then they could discuss Marv afterward.

Sitting in her kitchen at home, she dialed her best friend's phone number.

"Hi Mitzi, it's Sarah. I told you how my brother set me up with his friend, Marv, didn't I?"

"Yes, you did I'm so excited for you, just don't forget about your single best friend, you know, after you become a couple."

"That's exactly what I was thinking. I've mentioned Tim Lawrence to you, haven't I? He's handsome and funny and a great guy all around."

"If he's so great why aren't you dating him…oh, I forgot he's not Jewish."

"So, I was thinking that I could fix you up with Tim and we could make it a double date.

188

"I would love to go out with you and your new beau. And, Tim sounds dreamy," said Mitzy. "I can't wait to meet him."

"Oh, he is Mitzy. Tim is definitely dreamy. I'll pass along your number to him. I'll speak with you in a few days."

Hanging up the phone, Sarah took a deep breath, letting it out slowly. *I can do this. From this day on, Tim Lawrence is my friend and colleague and nothing more.*

Well, that wasn't as difficult as she thought it would be. Mitzi was extremely interested, after all. Now, Sarah had to propose the idea to Tim to her. Tim, though, might take a little more convincing.

"Tim, hi, it's Sarah. Don't worry; I'm not asking you out on a date, at least not with me. Remember my friend Mitzi? I believe I've mentioned her to you? I think I even showed you her picture."

"Yeah, I do. She's a real dish."

"Oh, I am so glad you think so."

"You are?" *Why are women so confusing?* he wondered.

"Yes, I am, because I'd like you and Mitzi to go out on a date." Tim was tickled. "Do Mitzi or I have a say in this, Sarah?"

"Of course, you do. I've already spoken to Mitzi, and she's all for it, and whether you admit it or not, I think you are too. I'll tell you what. Next week, I have a date with my brother Nate's friend, Marv. Why don't we all go out together? That way it won't be such a scary proposition for you."

"What makes you think I'm afraid to go out on a date with Mitzi? I'm a private investigator. Very little scares me."

"Okay, so if the big strong, brave man isn't scared, is it a date?"

"Yeah, it's a date." *Oh boy, what did he just agree to? Sarah and Mitzi at one time.* Could he handle it?

"Here's Mitzi's phone number, you ready? Gramercy 2-5080.

That's right. See you next Saturday night."

She looked forward to spending more time with Marv, Mitzi and Tim.

"Maybe I'll be able to bring a beau home that Bubbe would approve of," Sarah whispered to herself.

Bubbe peaked her head around the corner. "Mamala, I didn't mean to eavesdrop, but I think matching up Tim and Mitzi is a good choice. He sounds like a nice man and he's Catholic like Mitzi. Nate's friend, Marv, sounds like a much better match for you," her grandmother added. "I can't wait to meet him."

Oy, what have I gotten myself into now.

ACKNOWLEDGEMENTS

I have so many people to thank for supporting me while I wrote this book. First, a big shout-out to my writing cohorts Jackie Mendelson and Sharone Rosen, and my husband, Kenneth Kellogg, who joined our tribe a few years ago. They have all given me the fortitude, support, and objective critiques that were needed to make this story work. But it was the editing prowess of Nikki Basi that helped the story coalesce and take on its current form. I am tremendously grateful for her help.

ABOUT THE AUTHOR

Robin L.R. Kellogg has had a life-long love affair with the written word. Growing up in New Jersey, she knew that she wanted to write from a young age. In 1987 Robin relocated to Los Angeles, California. By 2000, she had founded Robin Kellogg Associates: offering copywriting, content, and ghostwriting services to help small businesses tell their story. Robin is also the creator of Author Your Book, a course that provides writers a safe space to develop their stories into books. She published her first nonfiction book, *A Life Put on Hold*, under the pen name Evie Rosen in 2014. An eBook, *12 Steps to Better Business Communications*, followed in 2016. *It All Began with a Goodbye* is her first novel.

Printed in the USA
CPSIA information can be obtained
at www.ICGtesting.com
LVHW050206090224
771345LV00002B/424

9 781684 986439